Coming Next Volume

Volume 4

Casey and Henry's journey through the Galar region continues! Casey is finally reunited with another of her missing Pokémon! Will she be able to find all of them? And can Henry win the challenge against Allister?!

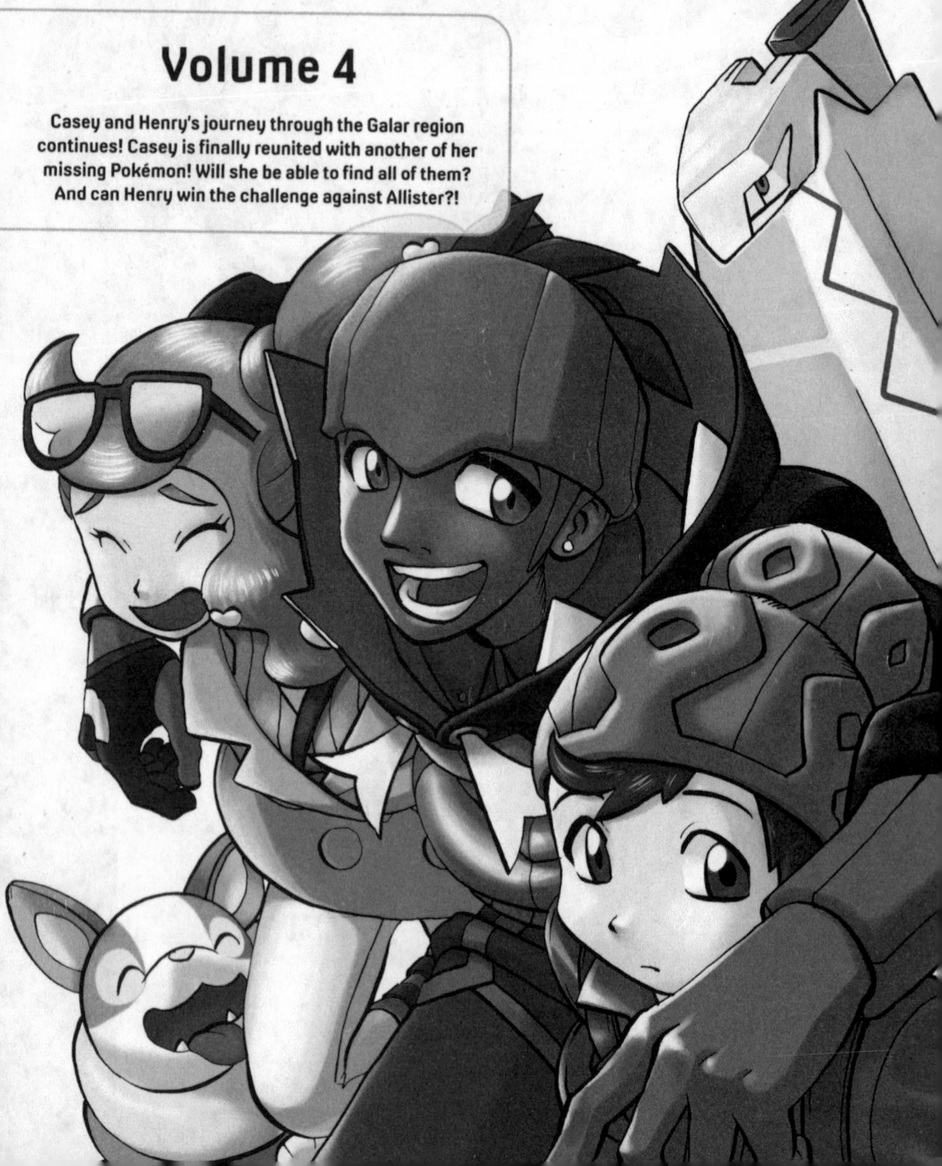

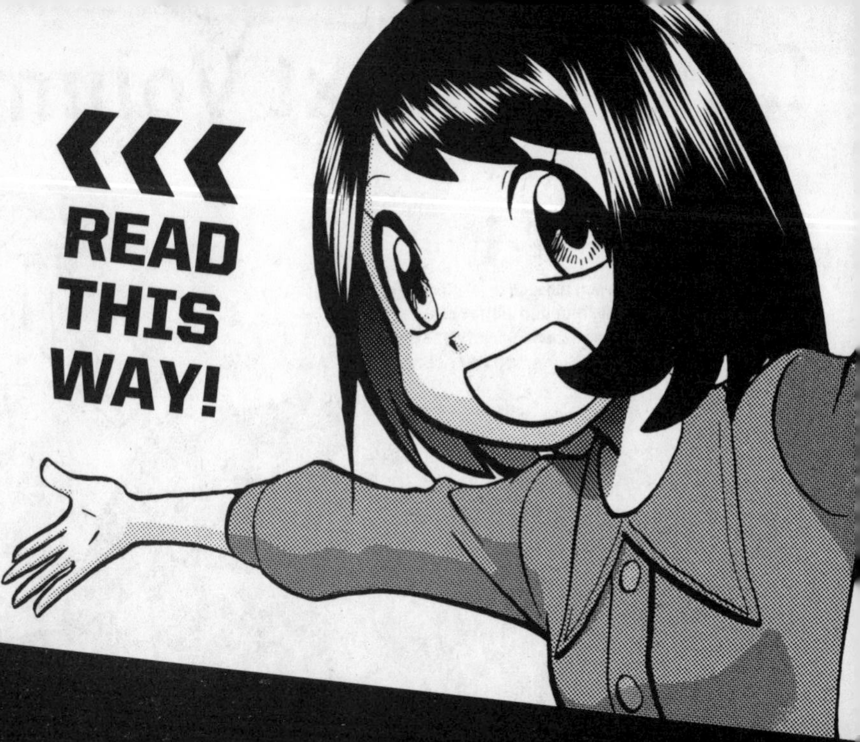
READ THIS WAY!

THIS IS THE END OF THIS GRAPHIC NOVEL!

To properly enjoy this VIZ Media graphic novel, please turn it around and begin reading from right to left.

This book has been printed in the original Japanese format in order to preserve the orientation of the original artwork. Have fun with it!

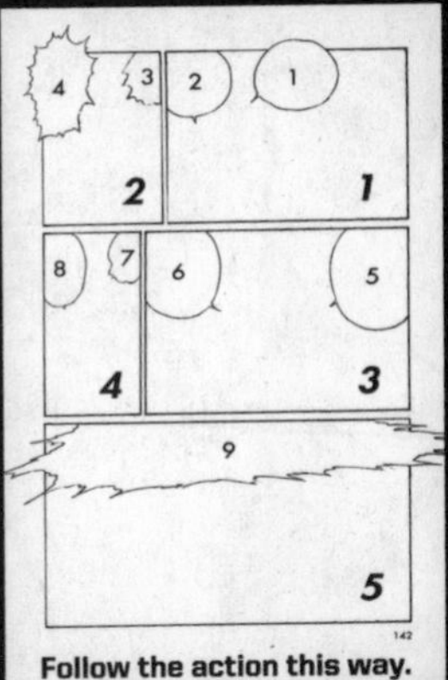

Follow the action this way.

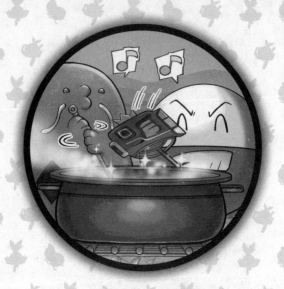

Hidenori Kusaka

I've completed my Curry Dex! I have been working hard to complete it, so I feel very satisfied about it. My favorite is Spicy Smoked-Tail Curry. Sounds so good! I hope you all try to record all 151 curries!

Satoshi Yamamoto

What I like best about *Pokémon: Sword & Shield*: ② Seeing Professor Magnolia's house in the distance when viewing the scenery from the top of the staircase in Wedgehurst. I love video games, manga, novels and music that do a great job of painting a beautiful landscape before you.

Pokémon™ Sword & Shield

3

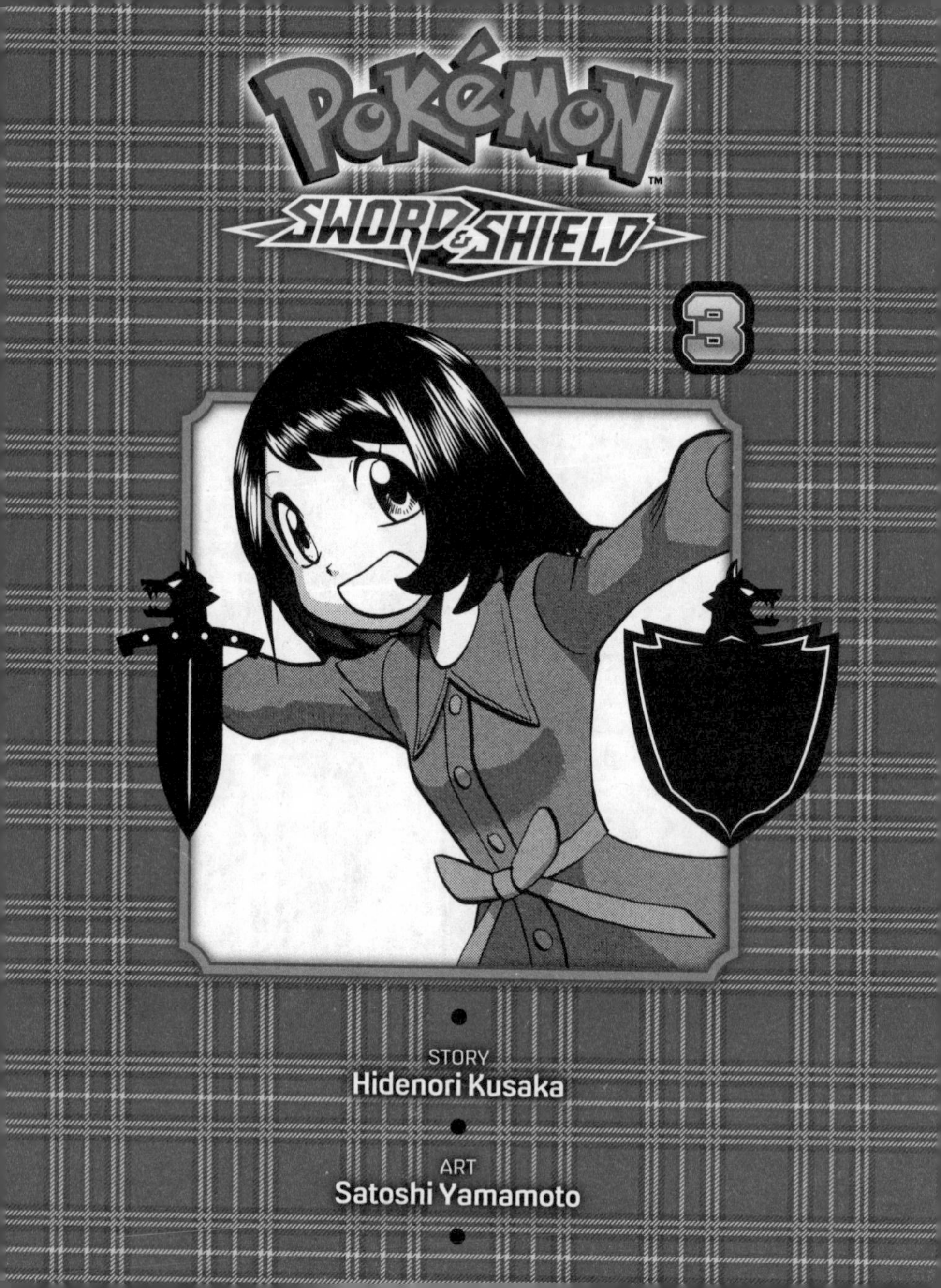

STORY
Hidenori Kusaka

ART
Satoshi Yamamoto

Henry
SWORD

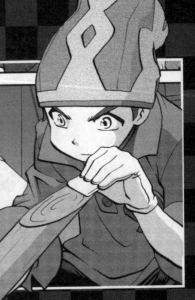

THE DESCENDANT OF A RENOWNED SWORDSMITH, HENRY IS AN ARTISAN WHO FIXES AND IMPROVES POKÉMON GEAR.

Casey
SHIELD

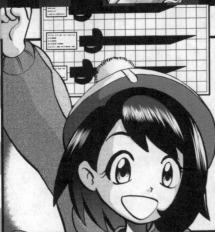

AN ELITE HACKER AND COMPUTER TECH WHO CAN ACCESS ANY DATA SHE WANTS. SHE'S PROFESSOR MAGNOLIA'S ASSISTANT AND TEAM ANALYST.

The Story So Far

UPON ARRIVING IN THE GALAR REGION, MARVIN SEES A DYNAMAXED POKÉMON AND FALLS OFF A CLIFF! HE IS SAVED BY HENRY SWORD AND CASEY SHIELD, AND JOINS THEM ON THEIR JOURNEY TO DISCOVER THE SECRET OF DYNAMAXING WITH PROFESSOR MAGNOLIA. HENRY AND CASEY ARE ALSO BEGINNING THEIR GYM CHALLENGE! THEIR JOURNEY CONTINUES AFTER THEIR FIRST GYM BATTLE AT TURFFIELD. WHAT'S NEXT FOR THEM?

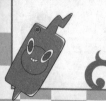

Marvin

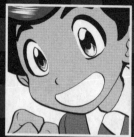

MARVIN'S A ROOKIE TRAINER WHO RECENTLY MOVED TO GALAR. HE'S EXCITED TO LEARN EVERYTHING HE CAN ABOUT POKÉMON!

Professor Magnolia

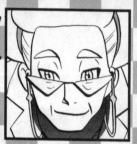

A FAMED RESEARCHER WHO STUDIES "DYNAMAXING," A.K.A. THE GIGANTIFICATION OF POKÉMON.

Leon

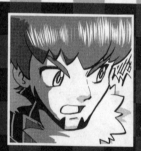

LEON IS THE BEST TRAINER IN GALAR. HE'S THE UNDEFEATED CHAMPION!

Sonia

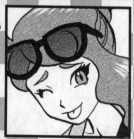

PROFESSOR MAGNOLIA'S GRAND-DAUGHTER AND LEON'S CHILDHOOD FRIEND. SHE'S HELPING THE PROFESSOR INVESTIGATE THE GALAR REGION!

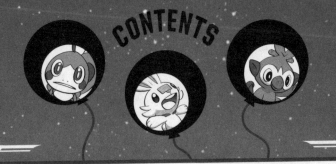

CONTENTS

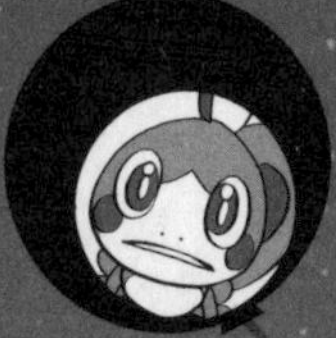

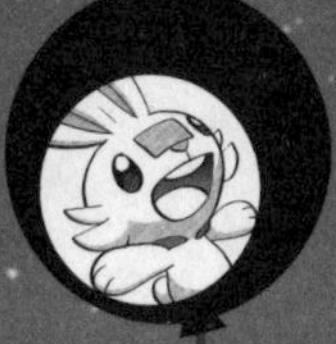

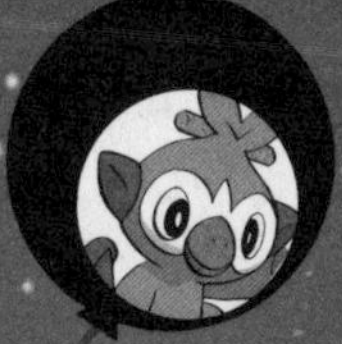

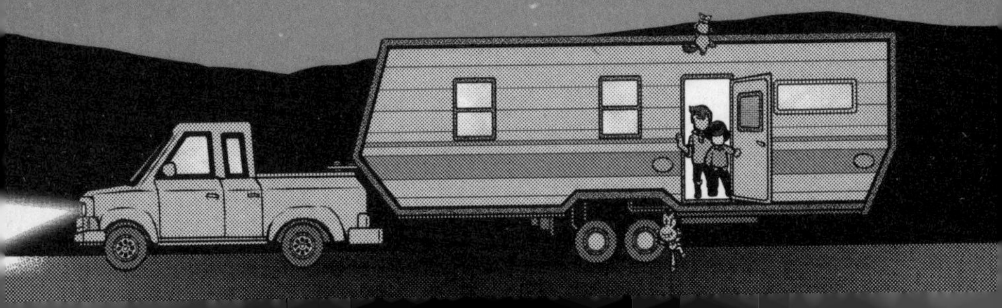

Adventure 8 Toasty!! Battle Against Toxapex

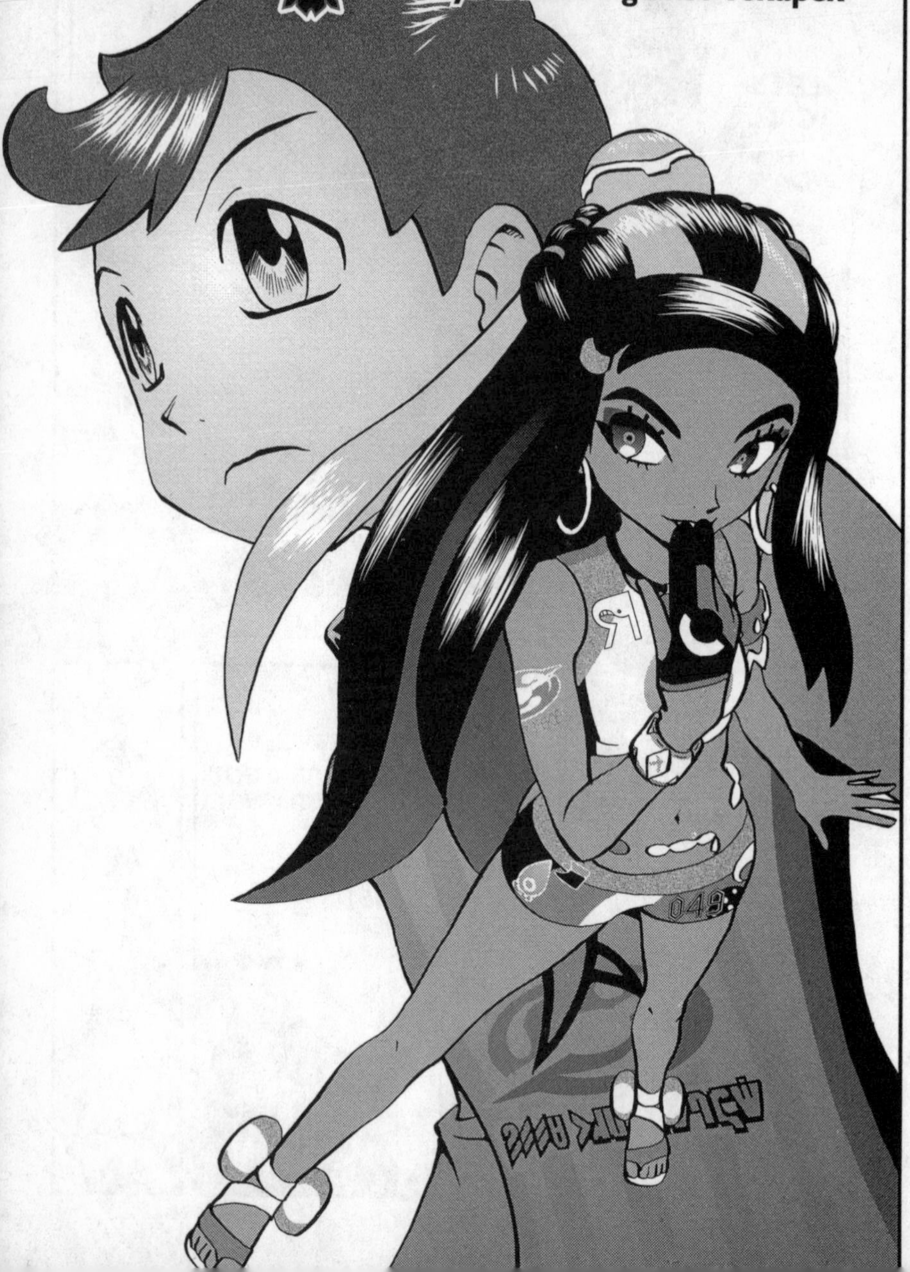
049

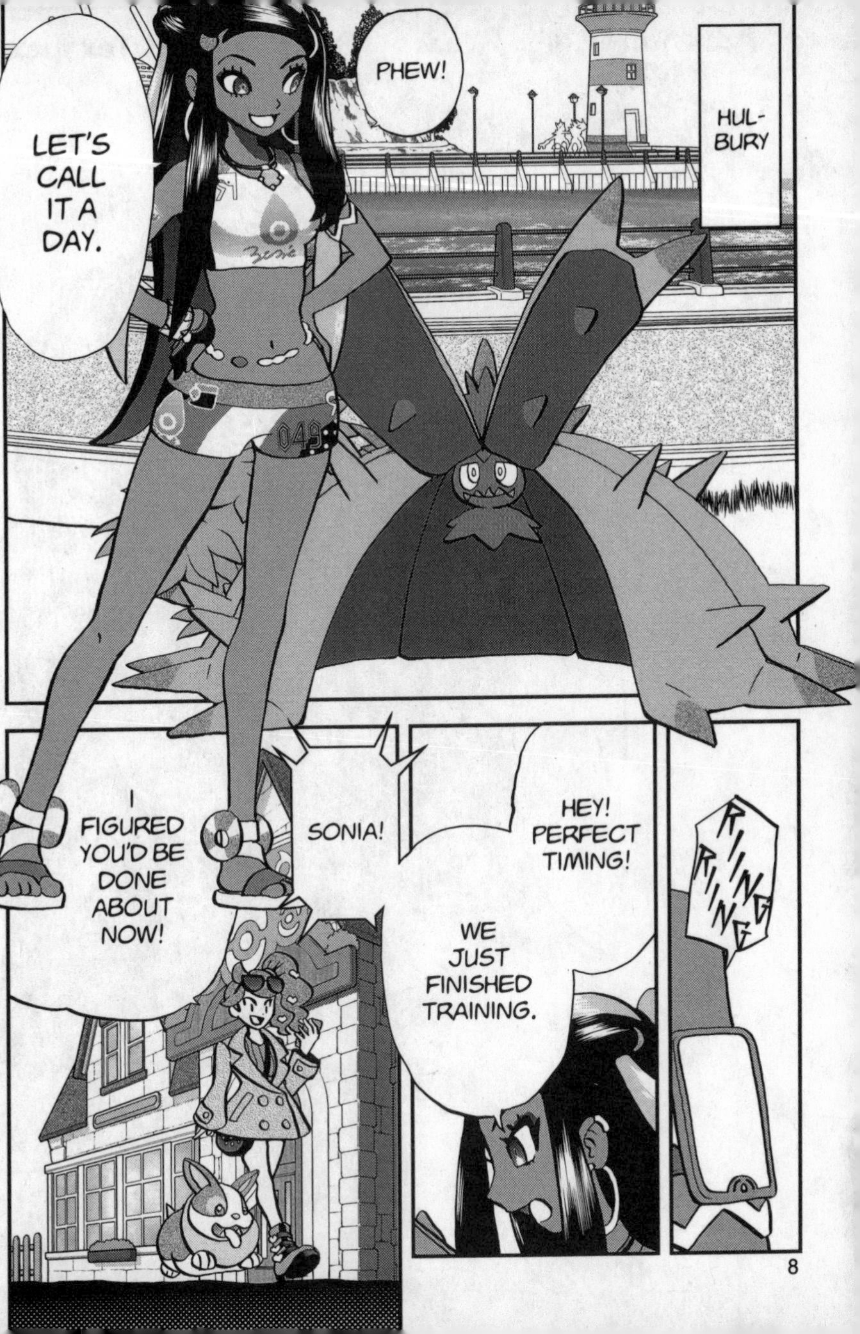
HUL-
BURY
PHEW!
LET'S CALL IT A DAY.
RING RING
SONIA!
HEY! PERFECT TIMING!
WE JUST FINISHED TRAINING.
I FIGURED YOU'D BE DONE ABOUT NOW!

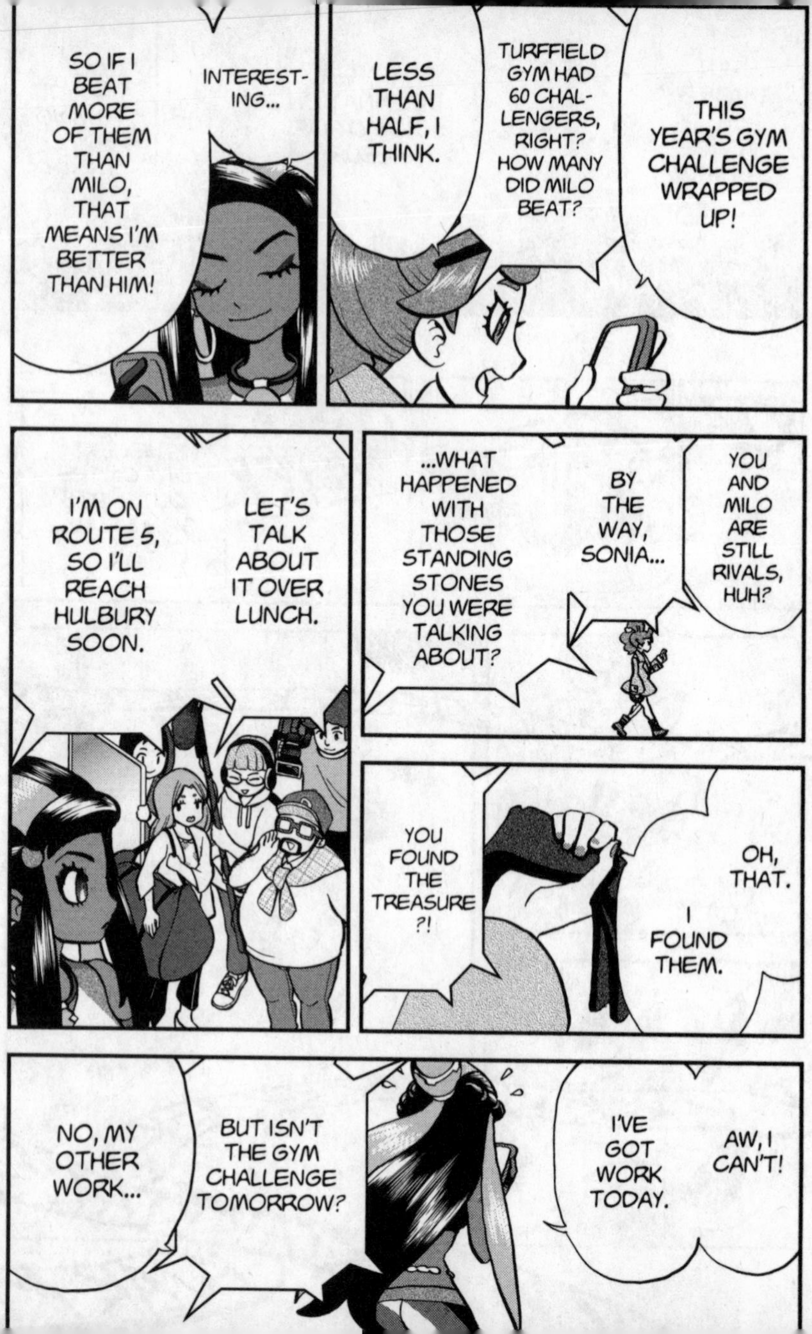
THIS YEAR'S GYM CHALLENGE WRAPPED UP!
TURFFIELD GYM HAD 60 CHALLENGERS, RIGHT? HOW MANY DID MILO BEAT?
LESS THAN HALF, I THINK.
INTERESTING...
SO IF I BEAT MORE OF THEM THAN MILO, THAT MEANS I'M BETTER THAN HIM!
YOU AND MILO ARE STILL RIVALS, HUH?
BY THE WAY, SONIA...
...WHAT HAPPENED WITH THOSE STANDING STONES YOU WERE TALKING ABOUT?
OH, THAT.
I FOUND THEM.
YOU FOUND THE TREASURE?!
LET'S TALK ABOUT IT OVER LUNCH.
I'M ON ROUTE 5, SO I'LL REACH HULBURY SOON.
AW, I CAN'T!
I'VE GOT WORK TODAY.
BUT ISN'T THE GYM CHALLENGE TOMORROW?
NO, MY OTHER WORK...

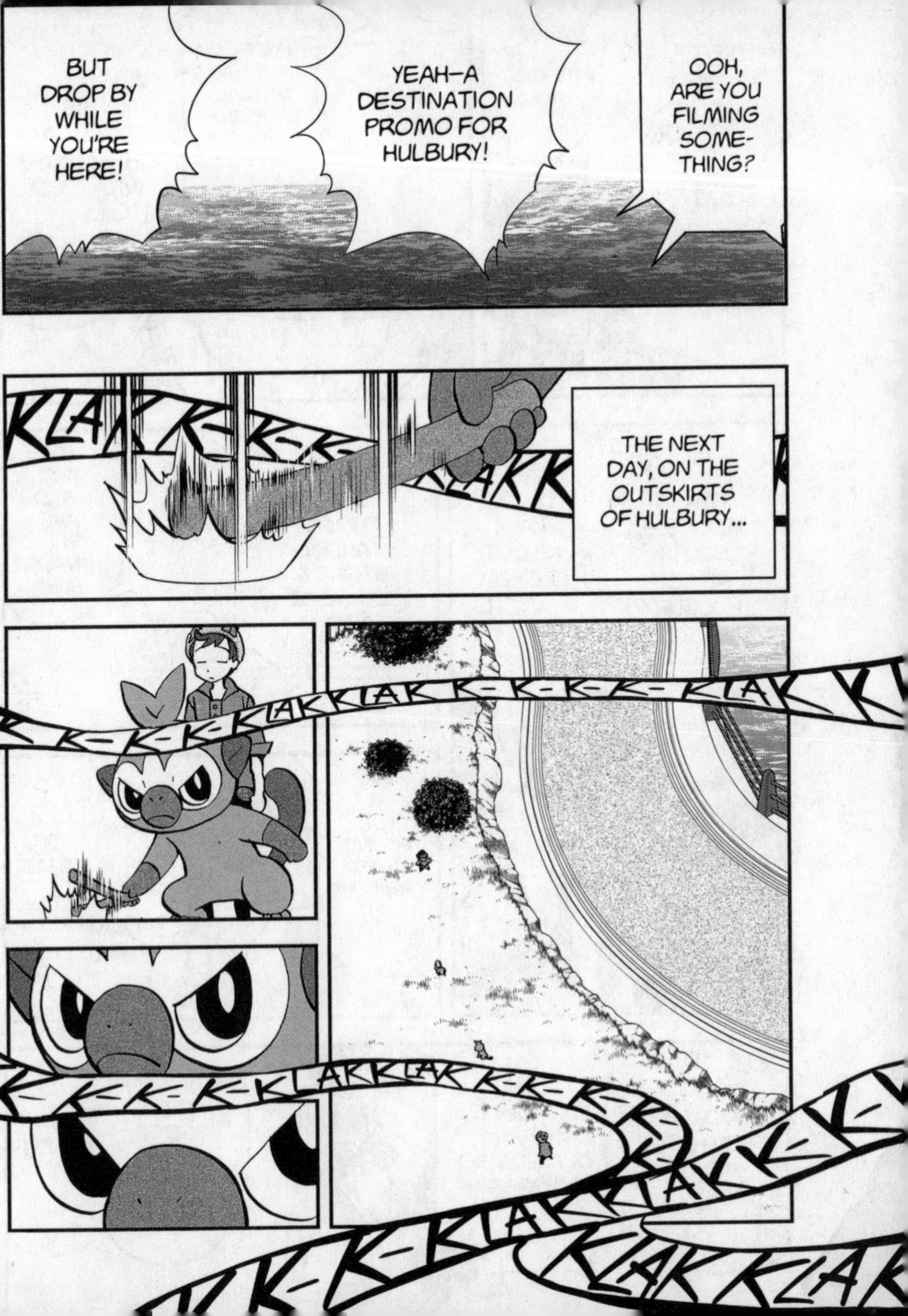
OOH, ARE YOU FILMING SOME-THING?
YEAH—A DESTINATION PROMO FOR HULBURY!
BUT DROP BY WHILE YOU'RE HERE!
THE NEXT DAY, ON THE OUTSKIRTS OF HULBURY...
KLAK K-K-K-KLAKK
KLAK K-K-K-K-KLAK
KLAKKLAK K-K-K-KRR
KLAKKLAK K-K-K-K-K-K-
KLAK KLAK

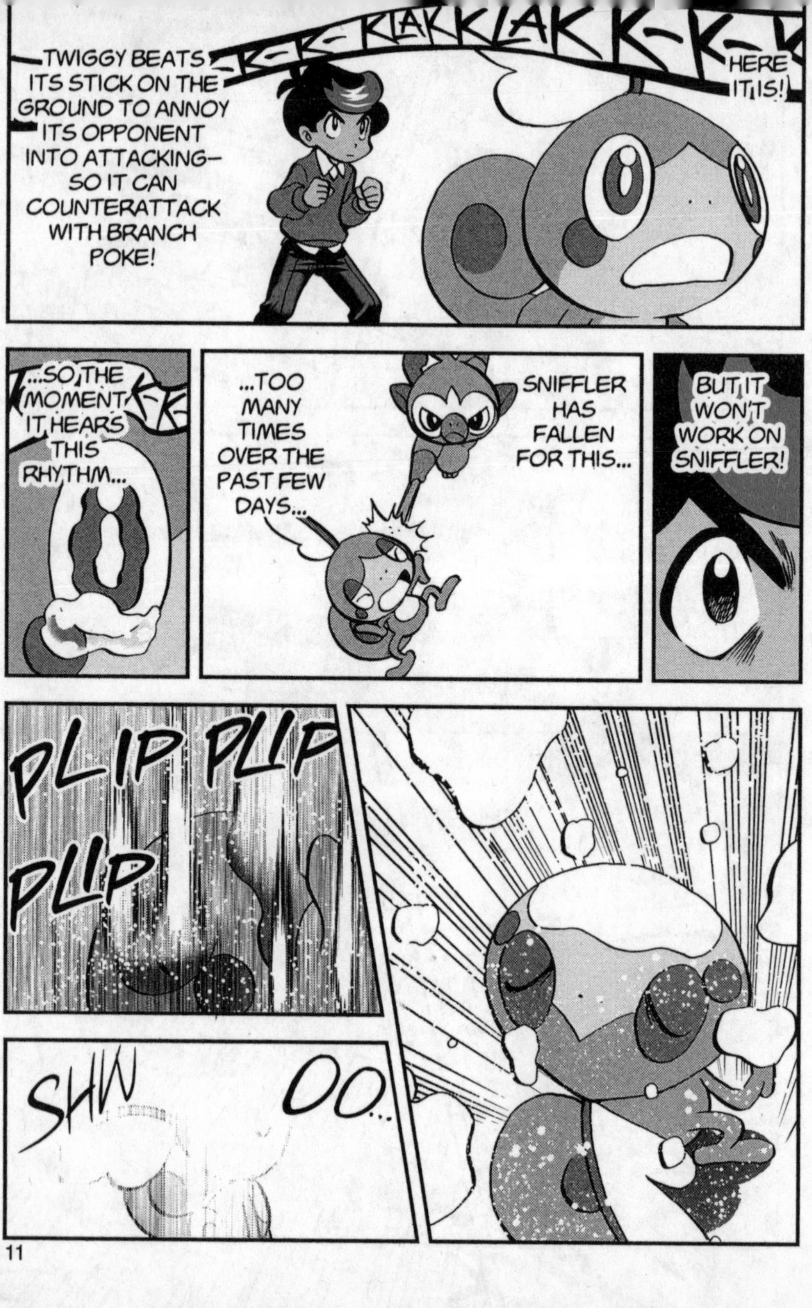
K-K-KLAK KLAK KLAK K-K-K
HERE IT IS!
TWIGGY BEATS ITS STICK ON THE GROUND TO ANNOY ITS OPPONENT INTO ATTACKING—SO IT CAN COUNTERATTACK WITH BRANCH POKE!
BUT IT WON'T WORK ON SNIFFLER!
SNIFFLER HAS FALLEN FOR THIS...
...TOO MANY TIMES OVER THE PAST FEW DAYS...
K-K
...SO THE MOMENT IT HEARS THIS RHYTHM...
PLIP PLIP PLIP
SHWOO...

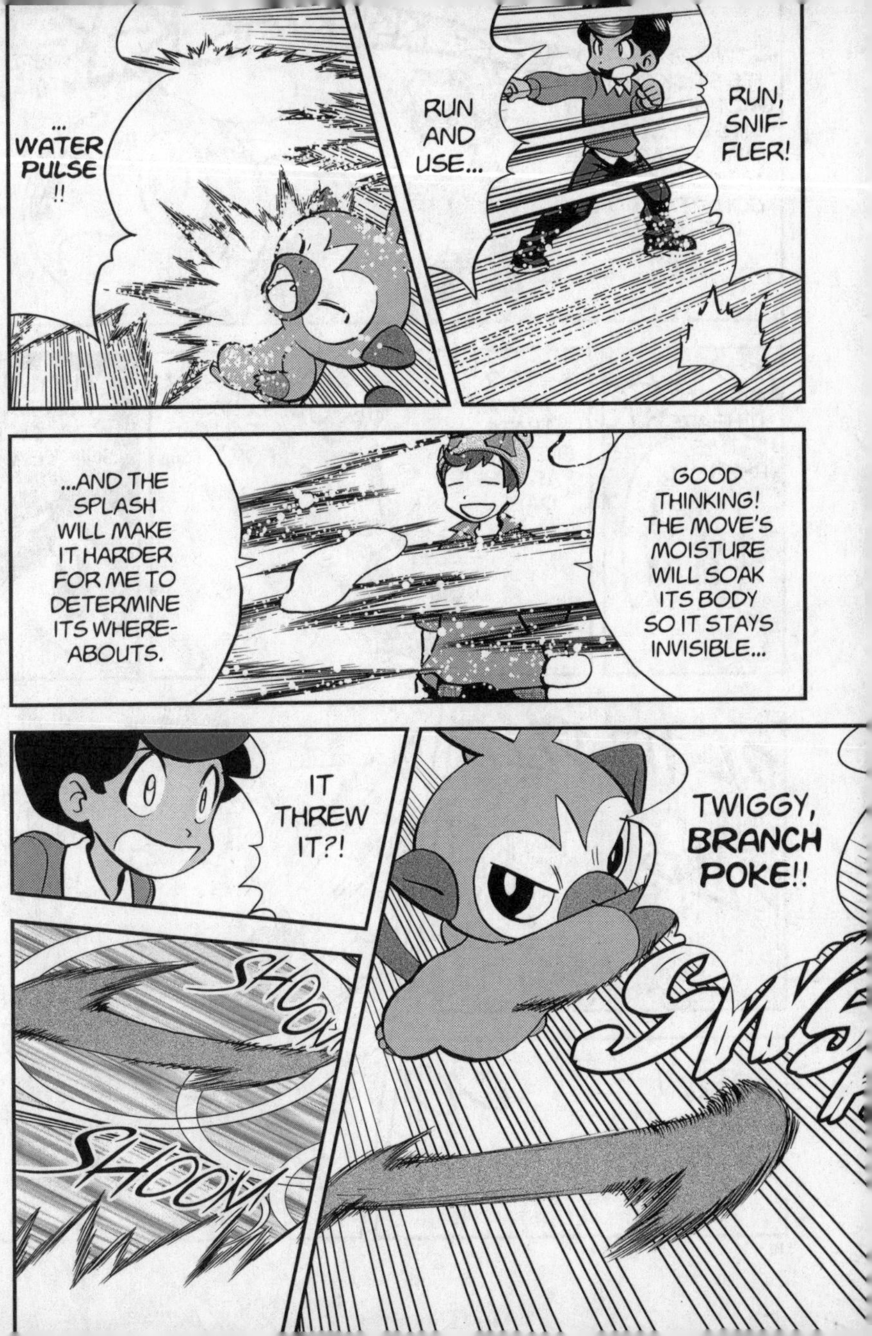
RUN, SNIF-FLER!
RUN AND USE...
...WATER PULSE!!
GOOD THINKING! THE MOVE'S MOISTURE WILL SOAK ITS BODY SO IT STAYS INVISIBLE...
...AND THE SPLASH WILL MAKE IT HARDER FOR ME TO DETERMINE ITS WHERE-ABOUTS.
TWIGGY, BRANCH POKE!!
IT THREW IT?!
SHOOM
SHOOM

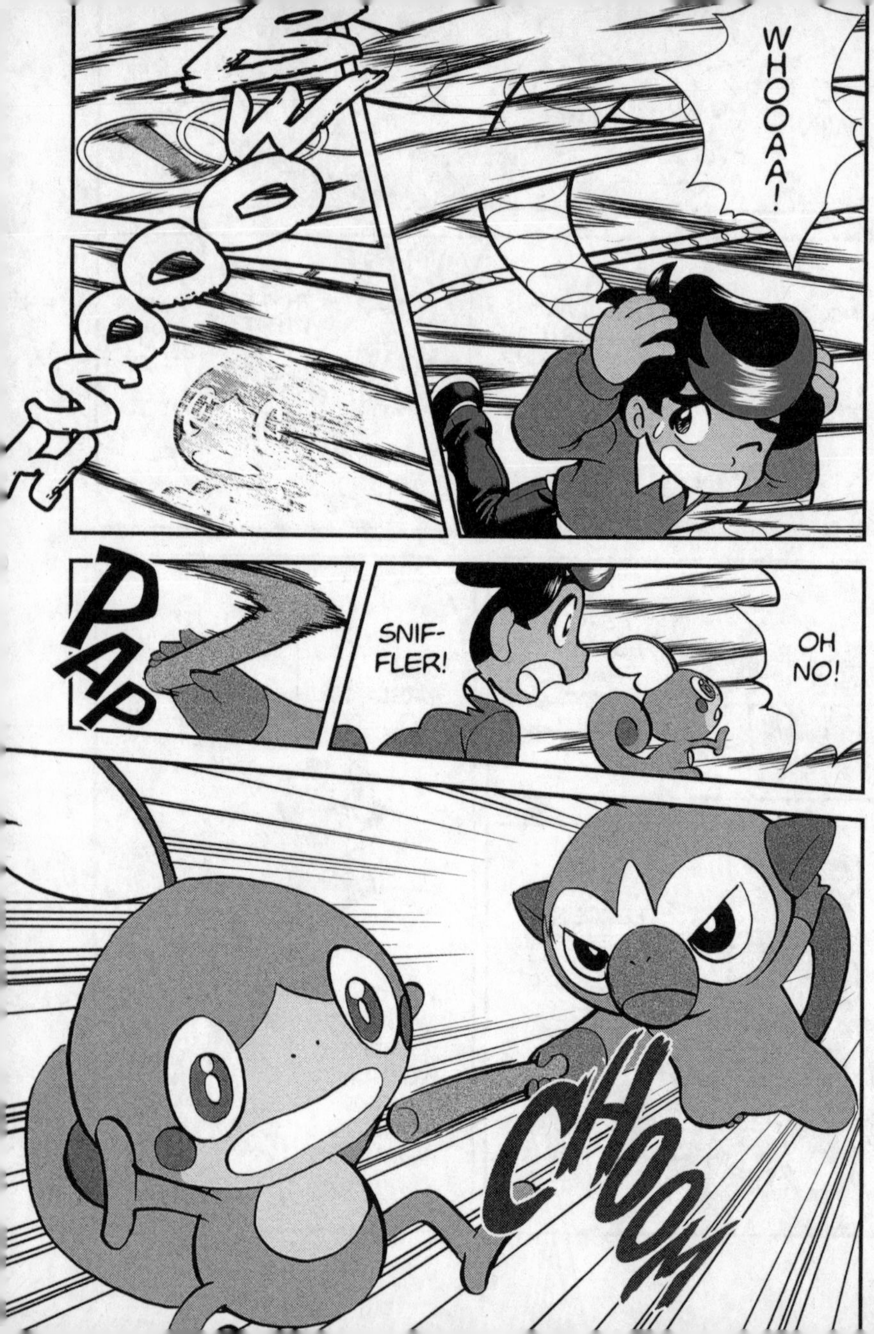
WHOOAAA!
BWOOOSH
OH NO!
SNIF-
FLER!
PAP
CHOOM

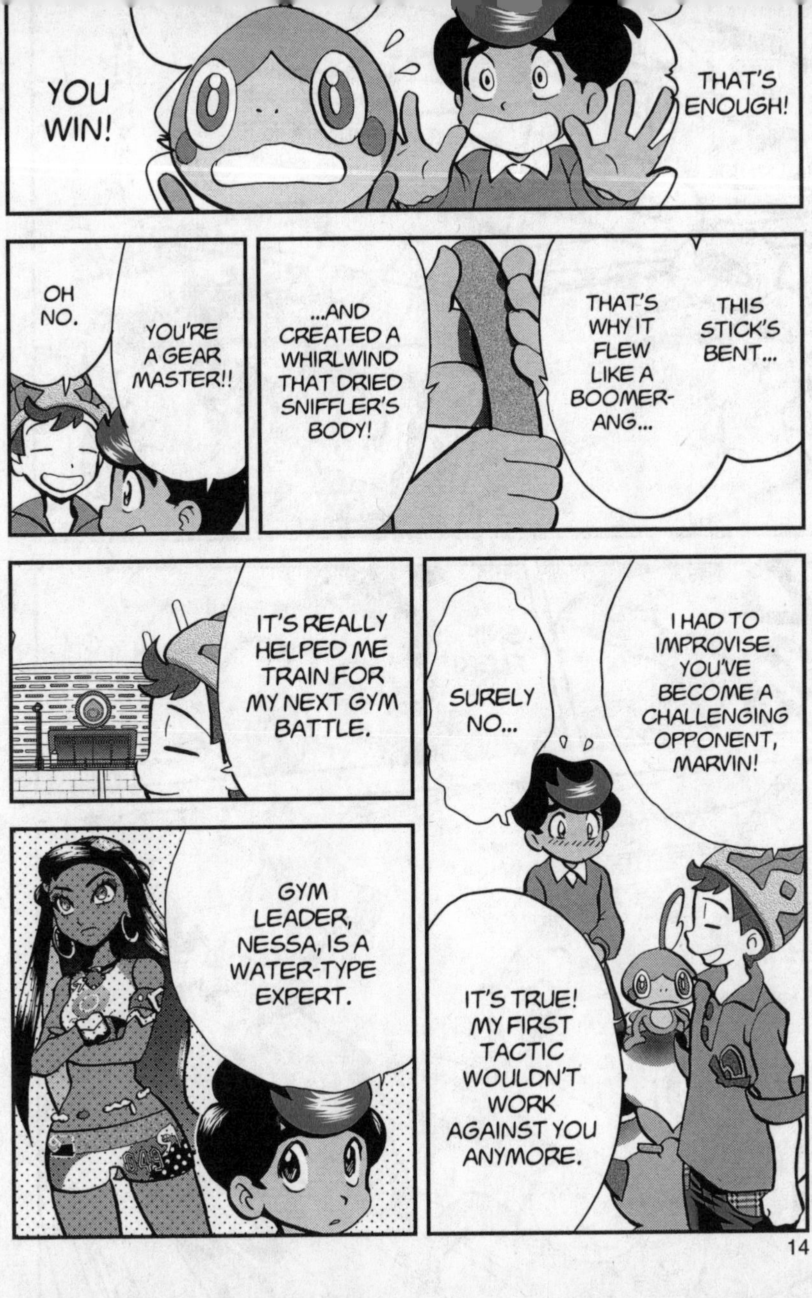
THAT'S ENOUGH!
YOU WIN!
THIS STICK'S BENT...
THAT'S WHY IT FLEW LIKE A BOOMER-ANG...
...AND CREATED A WHIRLWIND THAT DRIED SNIFFLER'S BODY!
YOU'RE A GEAR MASTER!!
OH NO.
I HAD TO IMPROVISE. YOU'VE BECOME A CHALLENGING OPPONENT, MARVIN!
SURELY NO...
IT'S TRUE! MY FIRST TACTIC WOULDN'T WORK AGAINST YOU ANYMORE.
IT'S REALLY HELPED ME TRAIN FOR MY NEXT GYM BATTLE.
GYM LEADER, NESSA, IS A WATER-TYPE EXPERT.

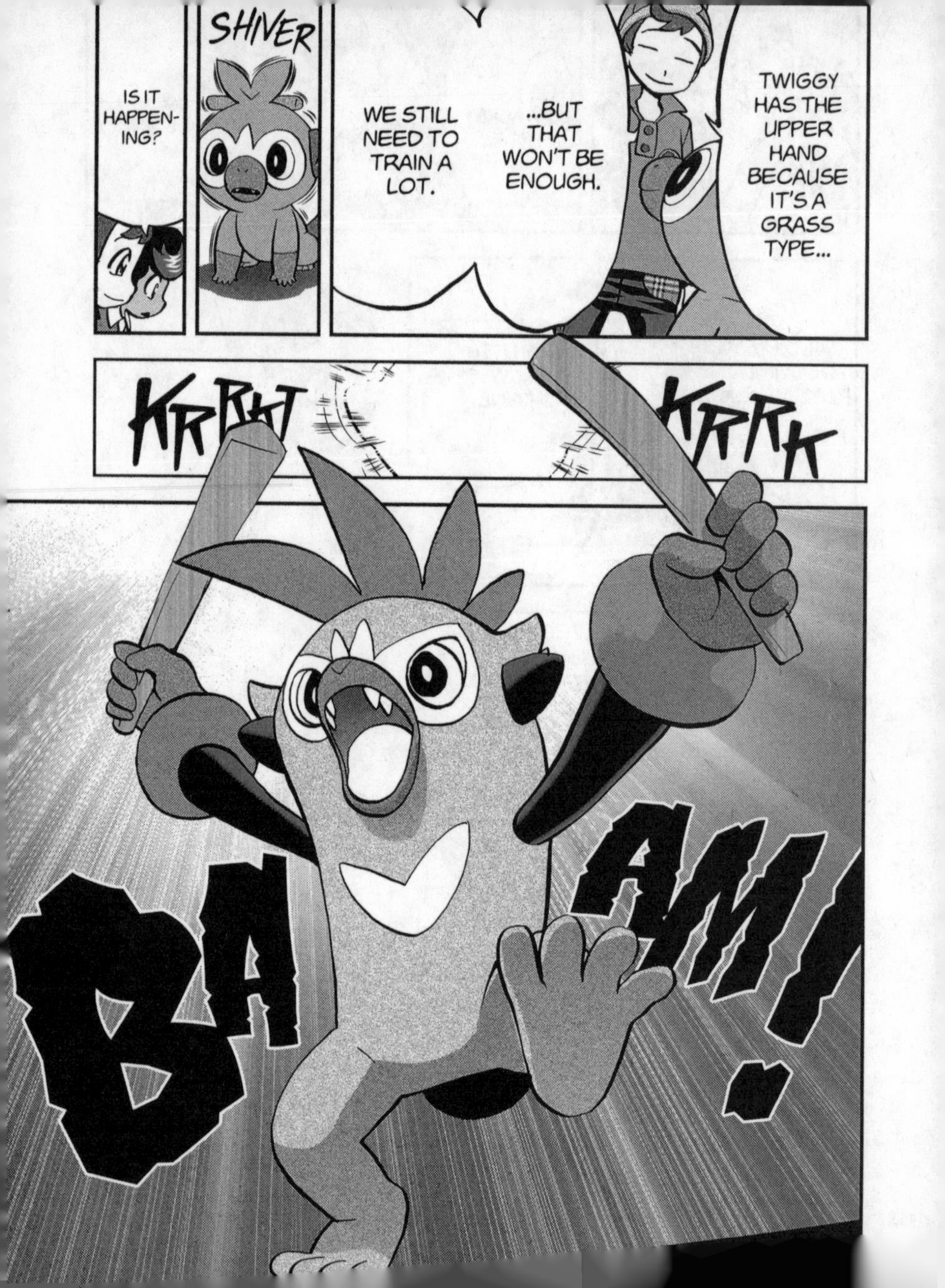
TWIGGY HAS THE UPPER HAND BECAUSE IT'S A GRASS TYPE...
...BUT THAT WON'T BE ENOUGH.
WE STILL NEED TO TRAIN A LOT.
SHIVER
IS IT HAPPEN-ING?
KRRK
KRRKT
BAAM!

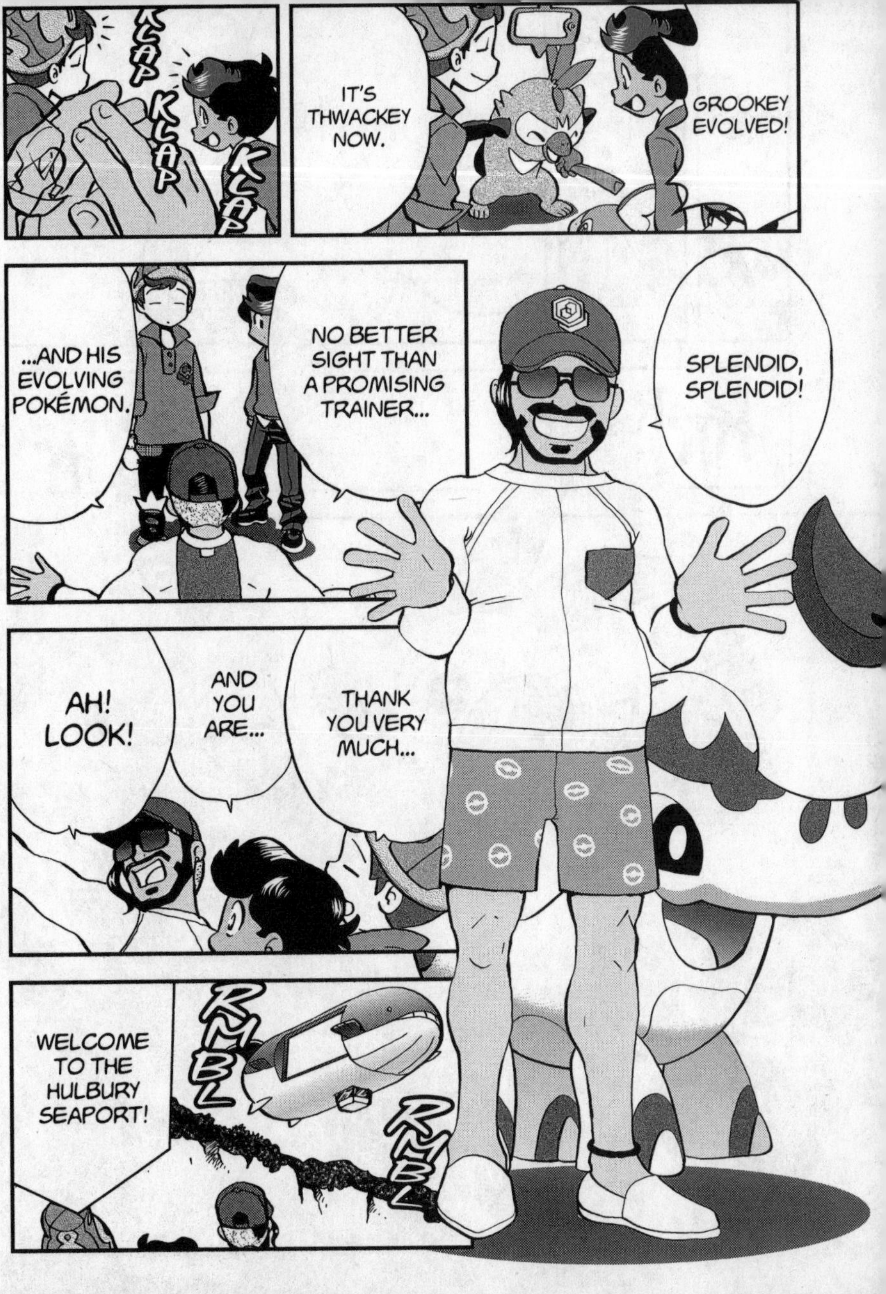
GROOKEY EVOLVED!
IT'S THWACKEY NOW.
KLAP
KLAP
KLAP
SPLENDID, SPLENDID!
NO BETTER SIGHT THAN A PROMISING TRAINER...
...AND HIS EVOLVING POKÉMON.
THANK YOU VERY MUCH...
AND YOU ARE...
AH! LOOK!
RMBL
RMBL
WELCOME TO THE HULBURY SEAPORT!

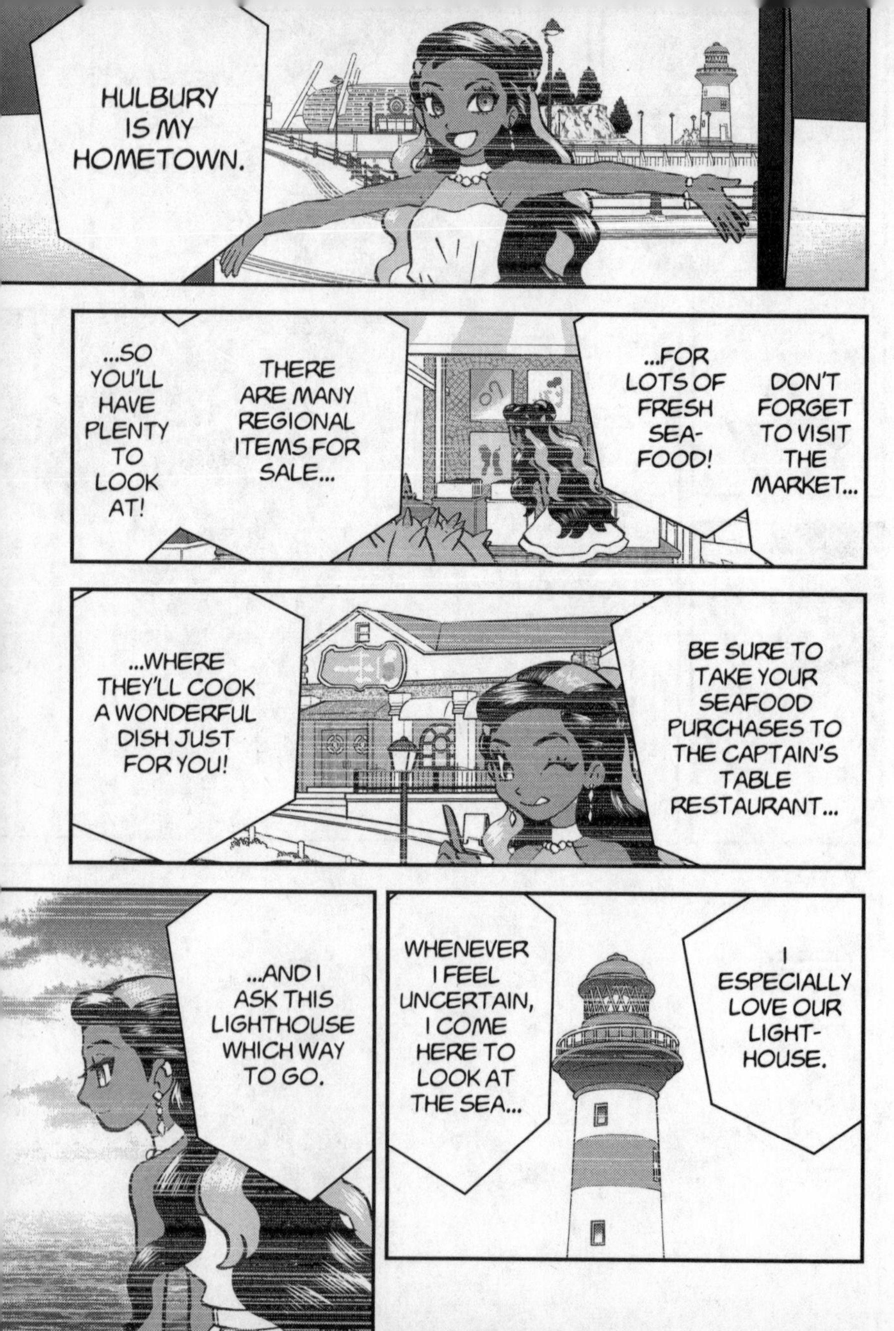
HULBURY IS MY HOMETOWN.
DON'T FORGET TO VISIT THE MARKET...
...FOR LOTS OF FRESH SEA-FOOD!
THERE ARE MANY REGIONAL ITEMS FOR SALE...
...SO YOU'LL HAVE PLENTY TO LOOK AT!
BE SURE TO TAKE YOUR SEAFOOD PURCHASES TO THE CAPTAIN'S TABLE RESTAURANT...
...WHERE THEY'LL COOK A WONDERFUL DISH JUST FOR YOU!
I ESPECIALLY LOVE OUR LIGHT-HOUSE.
WHENEVER I FEEL UNCERTAIN, I COME HERE TO LOOK AT THE SEA...
...AND I ASK THIS LIGHTHOUSE WHICH WAY TO GO.

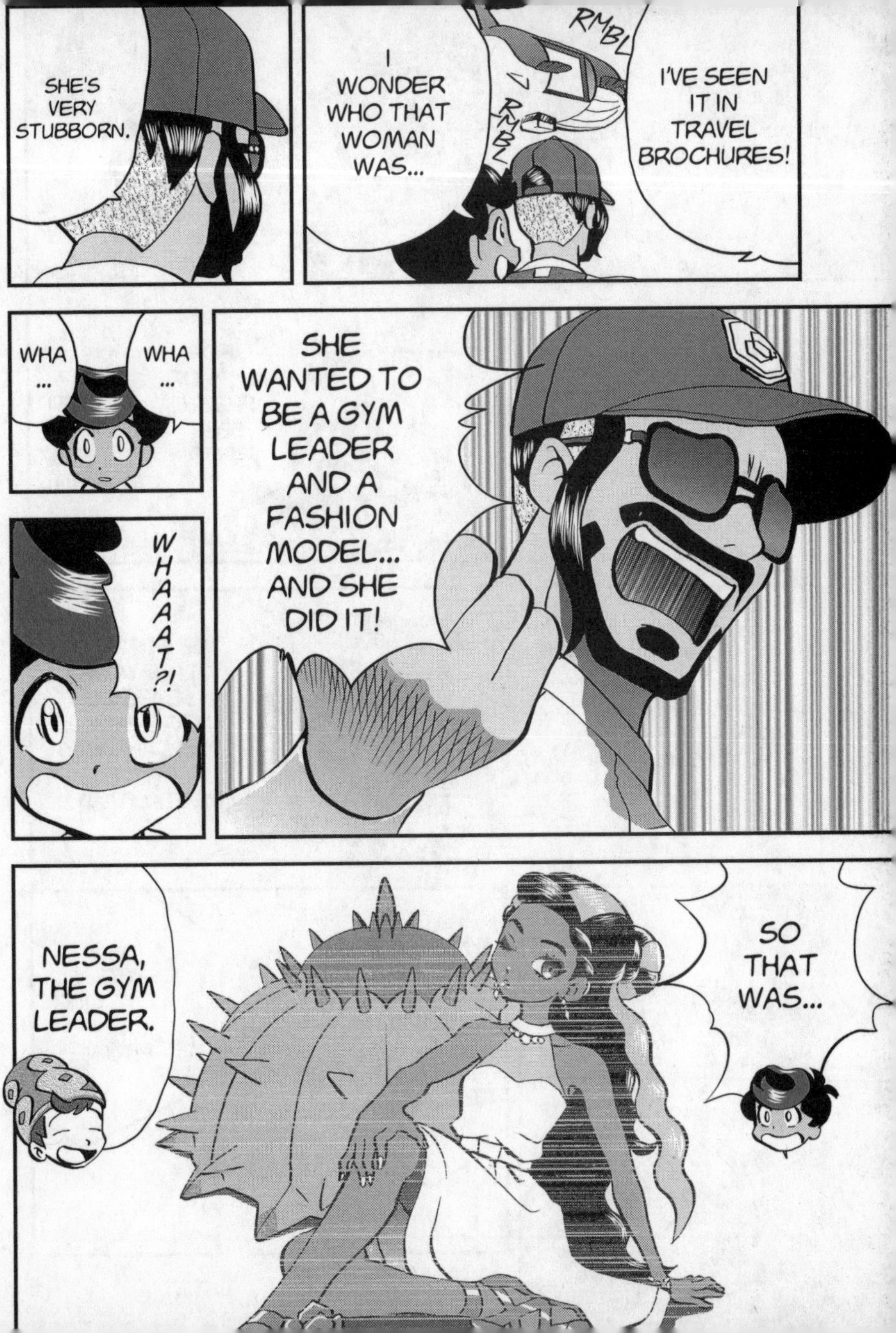
SHE'S VERY STUBBORN.
RMBL
I'VE SEEN IT IN TRAVEL BROCHURES!
I WONDER WHO THAT WOMAN WAS...
RMBL
SHE WANTED TO BE A GYM LEADER AND A FASHION MODEL... AND SHE DID IT!
WHA ...
WHA ...
WHAAAAT?!
SO THAT WAS...
NESSA, THE GYM LEADER.

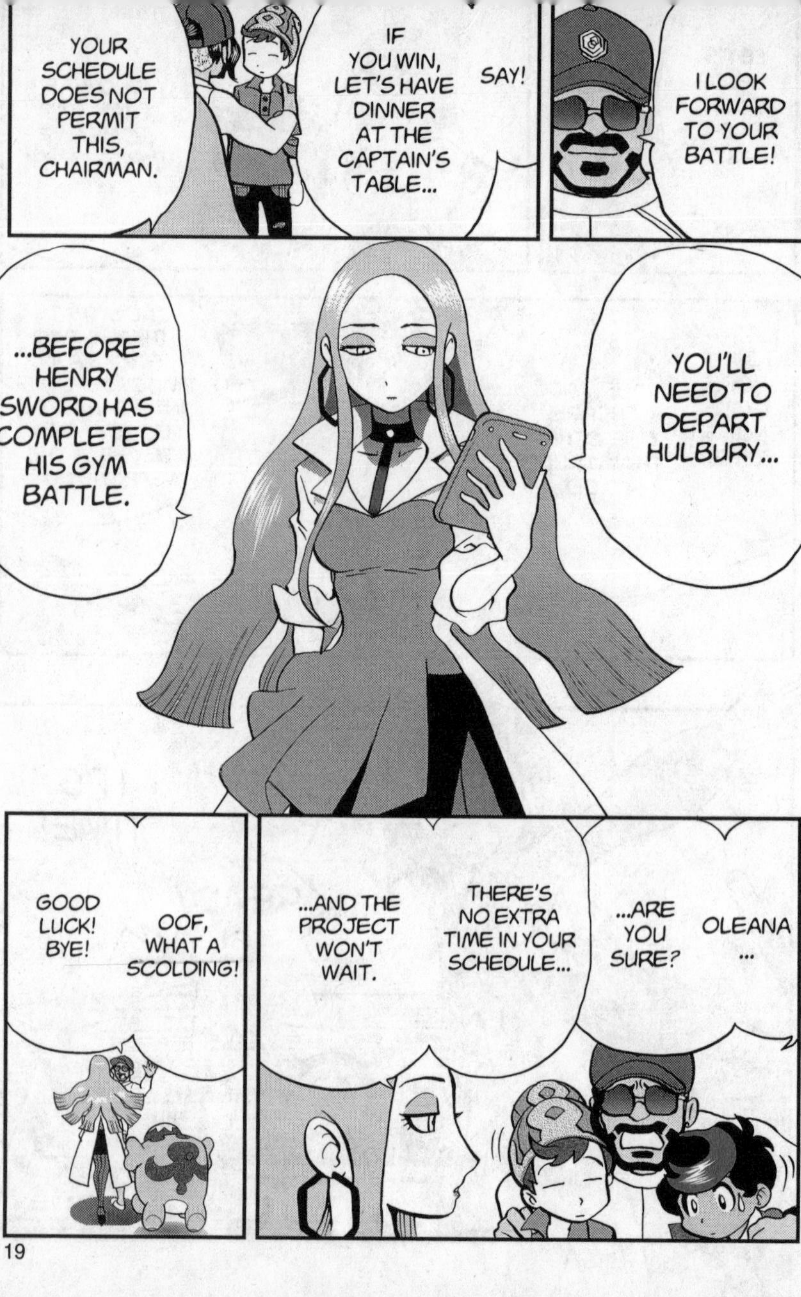
I LOOK FORWARD TO YOUR BATTLE!
SAY!
IF YOU WIN, LET'S HAVE DINNER AT THE CAPTAIN'S TABLE...
YOUR SCHEDULE DOES NOT PERMIT THIS, CHAIRMAN.
YOU'LL NEED TO DEPART HULBURY...
...BEFORE HENRY SWORD HAS COMPLETED HIS GYM BATTLE.
OLEANA ...
...ARE YOU SURE?
THERE'S NO EXTRA TIME IN YOUR SCHEDULE...
...AND THE PROJECT WON'T WAIT.
OOF, WHAT A SCOLDING!
GOOD LUCK! BYE!

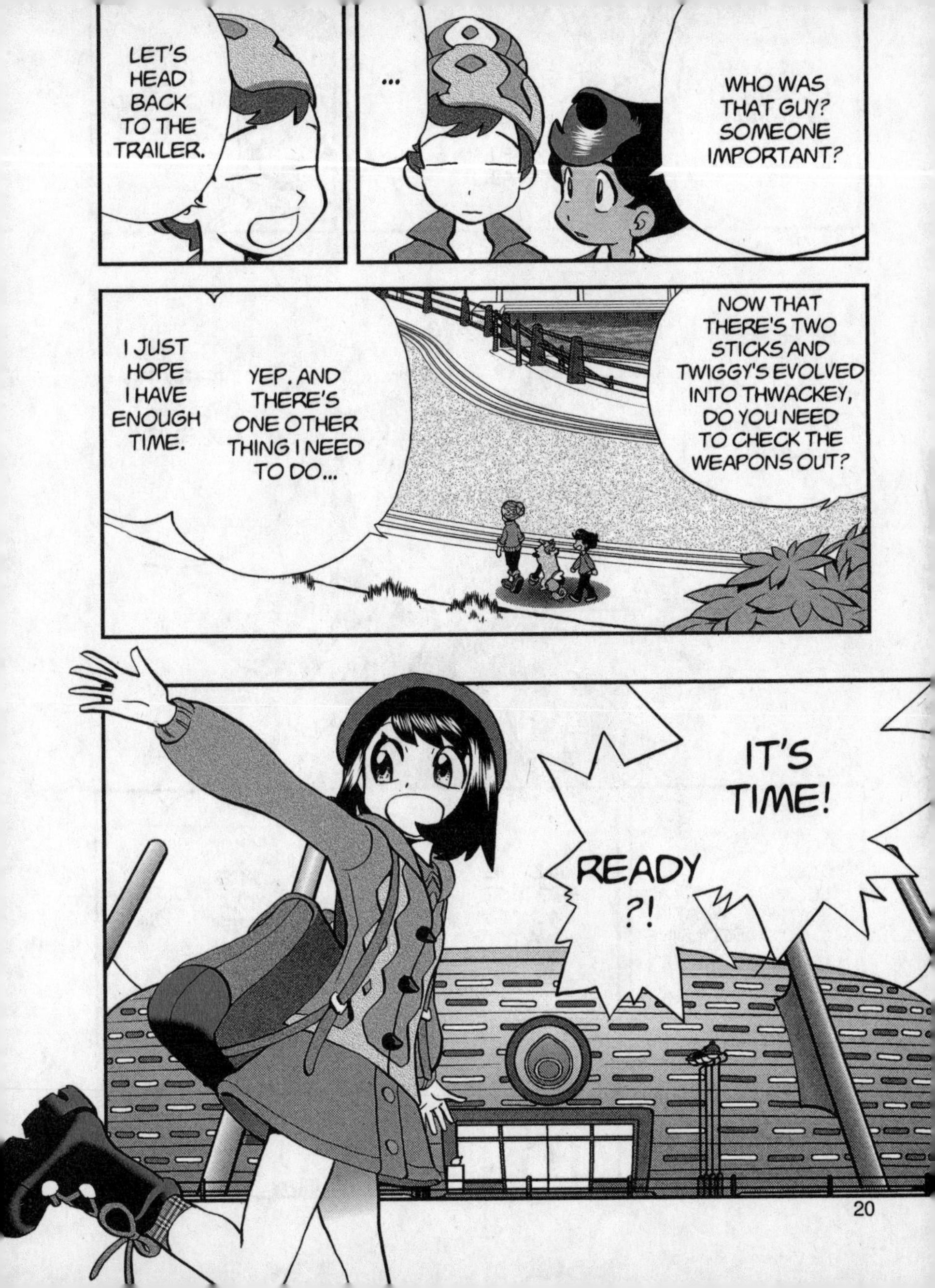
WHO WAS THAT GUY? SOMEONE IMPORTANT?
...
LET'S HEAD BACK TO THE TRAILER.
NOW THAT THERE'S TWO STICKS AND TWIGGY'S EVOLVED INTO THWACKEY, DO YOU NEED TO CHECK THE WEAPONS OUT?
YEP. AND THERE'S ONE OTHER THING I NEED TO DO...
I JUST HOPE I HAVE ENOUGH TIME.
IT'S TIME!
READY ?!

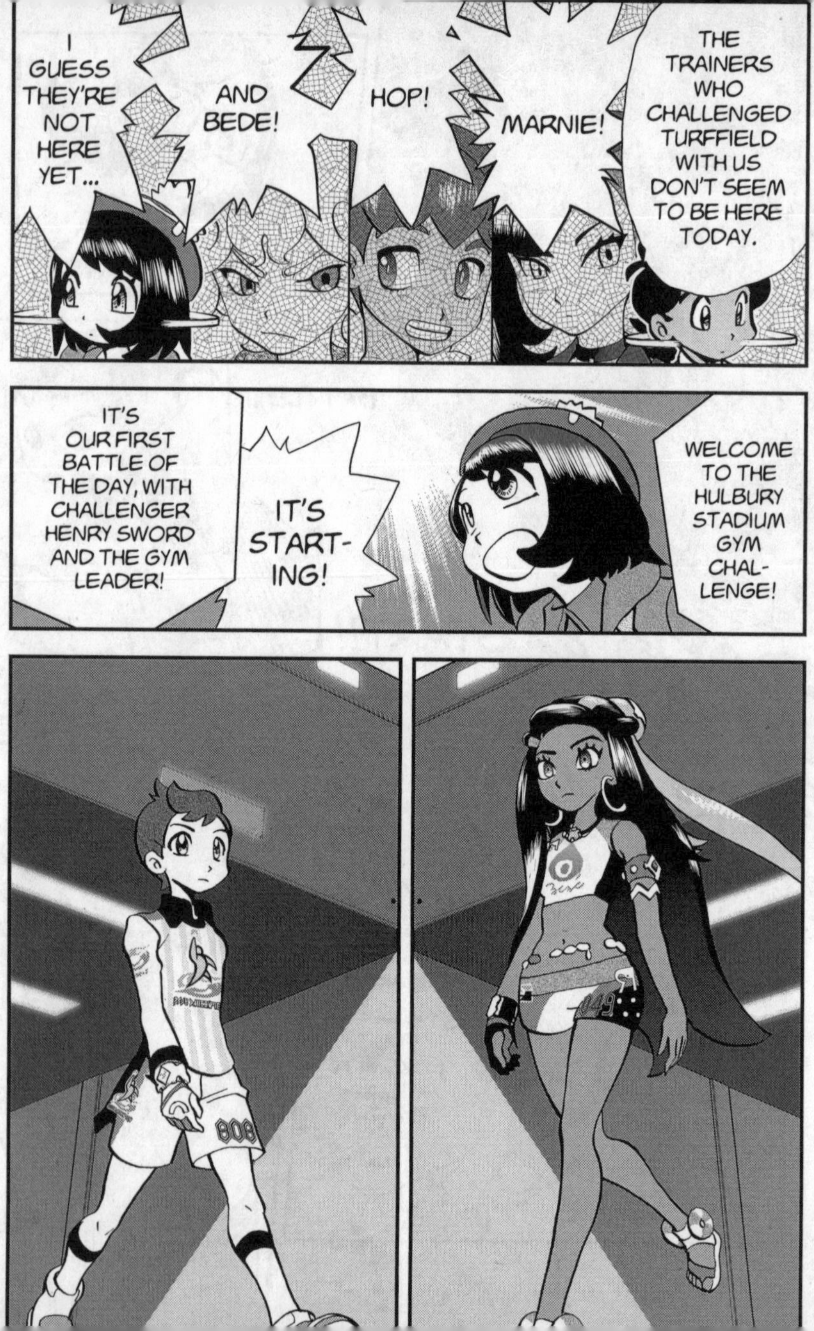
THE TRAINERS WHO CHALLENGED TURFFIELD WITH US DON'T SEEM TO BE HERE TODAY.
MARNIE!
HOP!
AND BEDE!
I GUESS THEY'RE NOT HERE YET...
WELCOME TO THE HULBURY STADIUM GYM CHAL-LENGE!
IT'S START-ING!
IT'S OUR FIRST BATTLE OF THE DAY, WITH CHALLENGER HENRY SWORD AND THE GYM LEADER!

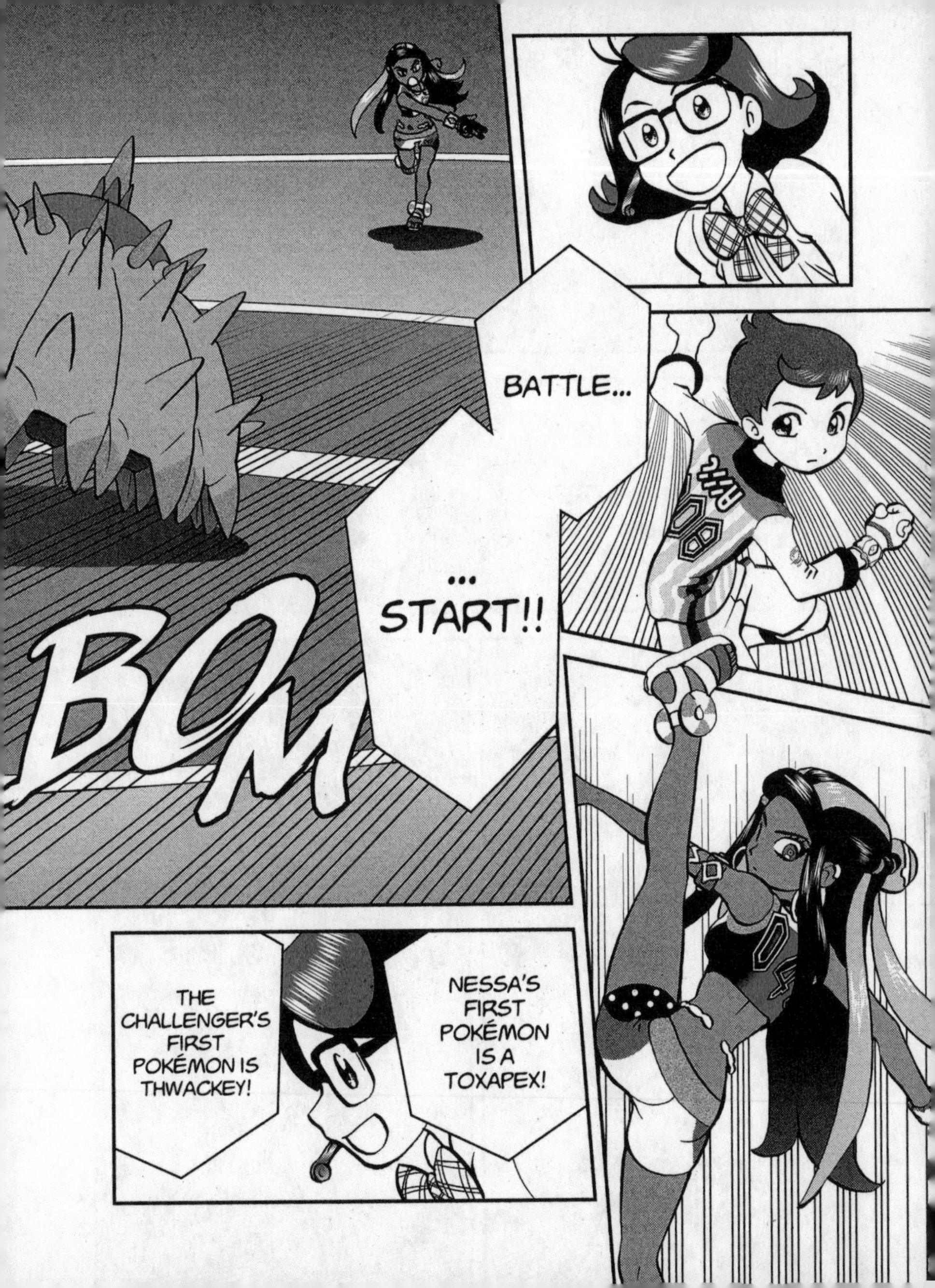
BATTLE...
... START!!
BOM
NESSA'S FIRST POKÉMON IS A TOXAPEX!
THE CHALLENGER'S FIRST POKÉMON IS THWACKEY!

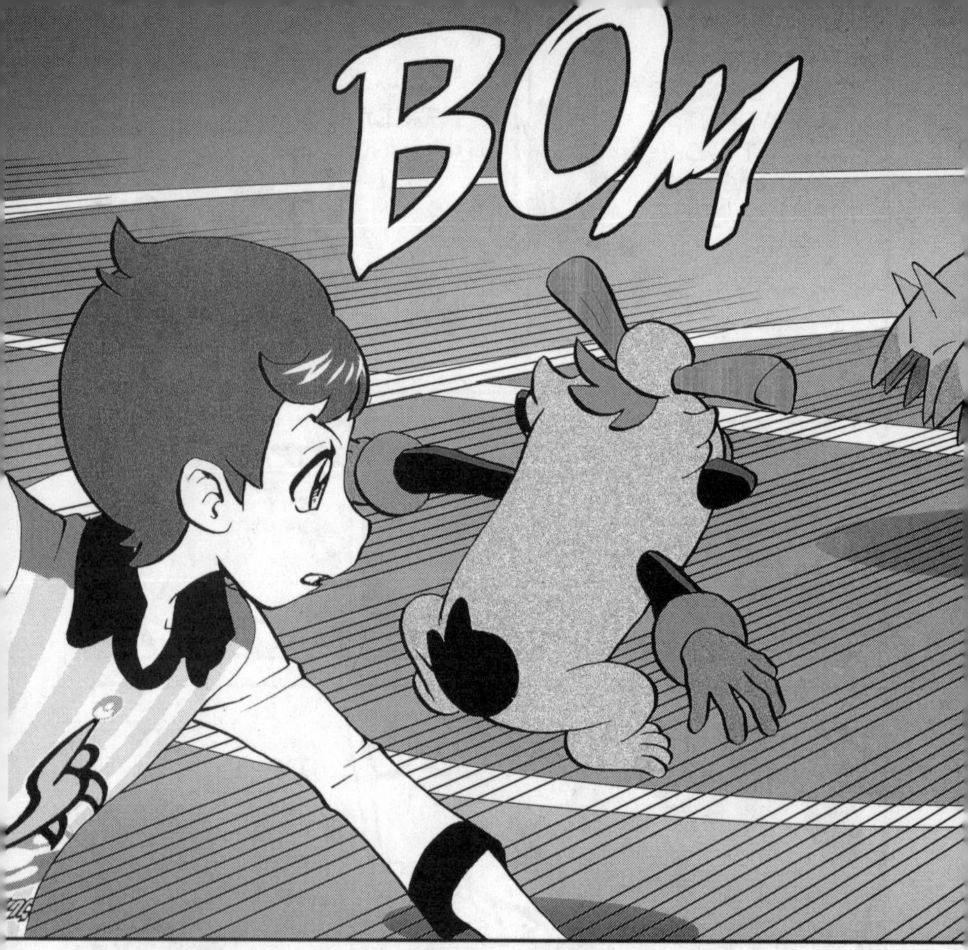
BOM

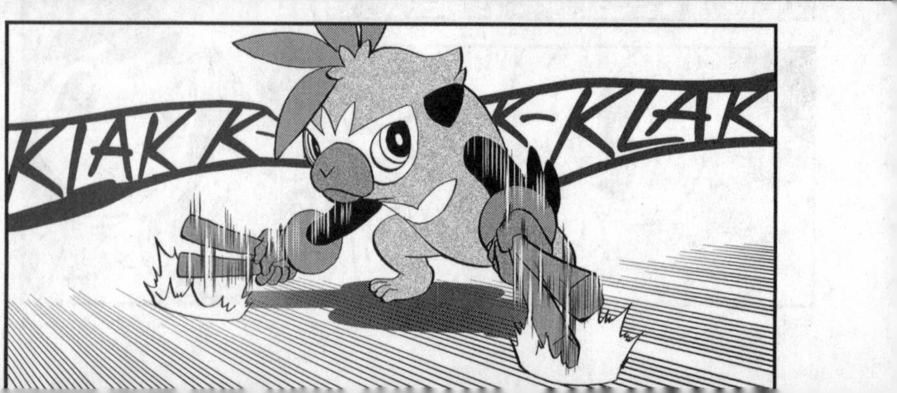
KLAK K-
K-KLAK

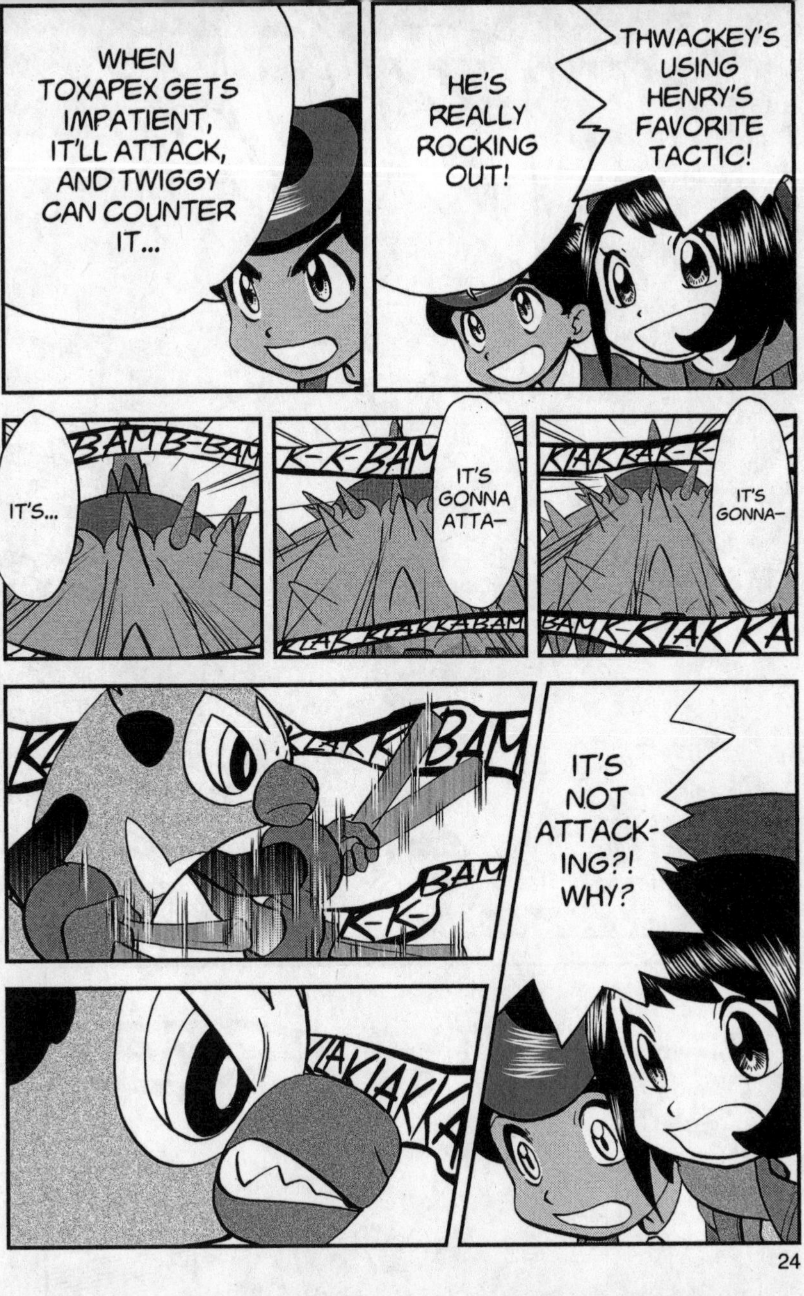
THWACKEY'S USING HENRY'S FAVORITE TACTIC!
HE'S REALLY ROCKING OUT!
WHEN TOXAPEX GETS IMPATIENT, IT'LL ATTACK, AND TWIGGY CAN COUNTER IT...
IT'S GONNA-
BAMK-KLAKKA
IT'S GONNA ATTA-
K-K-BAM
BAMB-BAM
IT'S...
IT'S NOT ATTACKING?! WHY?
BAM
BAM
K-K-

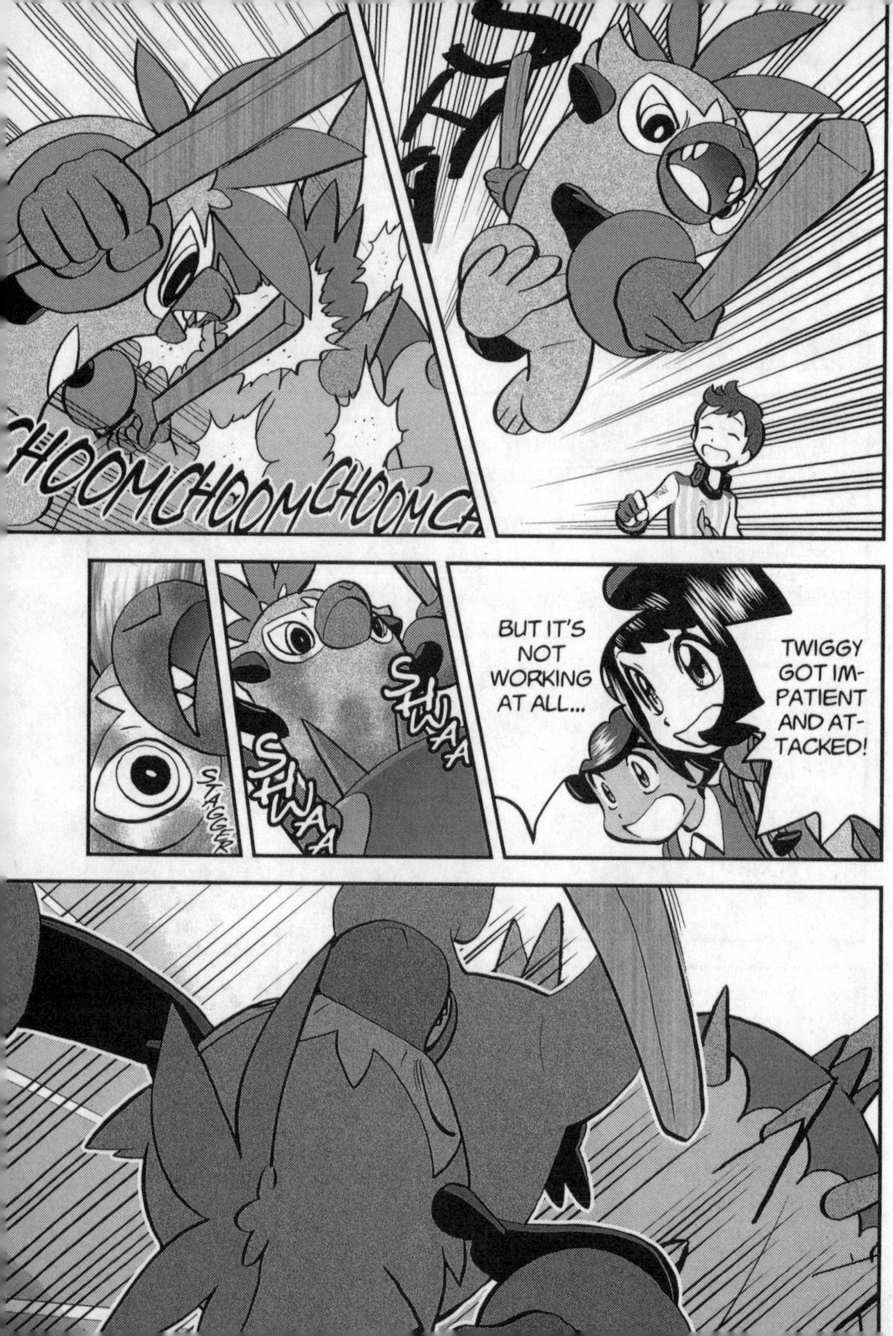
CHOOMCHOOMCHOOM
TWIGGY GOT IM-PATIENT AND AT-TACKED!
BUT IT'S NOT WORKING AT ALL...
SHWAA
SHWAA
STAGGER

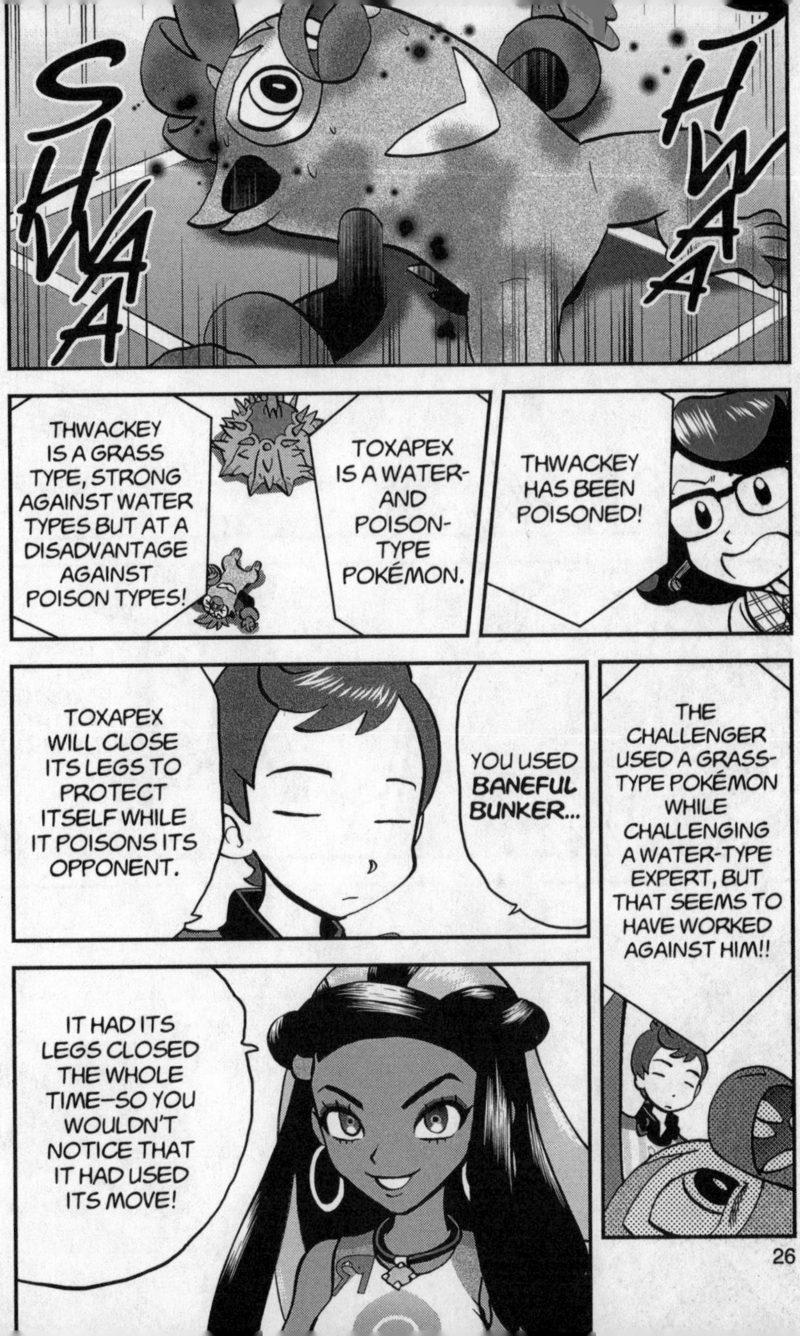
SHWAA
SHWAA
THWACKEY HAS BEEN POISONED!
TOXAPEX IS A WATER- AND POISON-TYPE POKÉMON.
THWACKEY IS A GRASS TYPE, STRONG AGAINST WATER TYPES BUT AT A DISADVANTAGE AGAINST POISON TYPES!
THE CHALLENGER USED A GRASS-TYPE POKÉMON WHILE CHALLENGING A WATER-TYPE EXPERT, BUT THAT SEEMS TO HAVE WORKED AGAINST HIM!!
YOU USED **BANEFUL BUNKER**...
TOXAPEX WILL CLOSE ITS LEGS TO PROTECT ITSELF WHILE IT POISONS ITS OPPONENT.
IT HAD ITS LEGS CLOSED THE WHOLE TIME—SO YOU WOULDN'T NOTICE THAT IT HAD USED ITS MOVE!

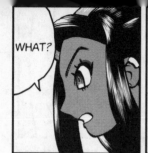

WHAT?

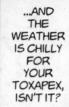

...AND THE WEATHER IS CHILLY FOR YOUR TOXAPEX, ISN'T IT?

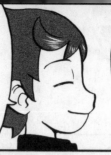

HULBURY HAS COLD WATER...

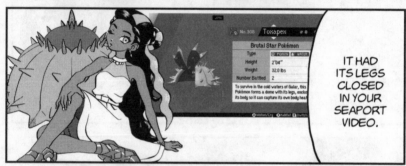

No.308	Тохарех	
Brutal Star Pokémon		
Type	POISON	WATER
Height	2'04"	
Weight	32.0 lbs	
Number Battled	2	

To survive in the cold waters of Galar, this Pokémon forms a dome with its legs, enclosing its body so it can capture its own body heat.

IT HAD ITS LEGS CLOSED IN YOUR SEAPORT VIDEO.

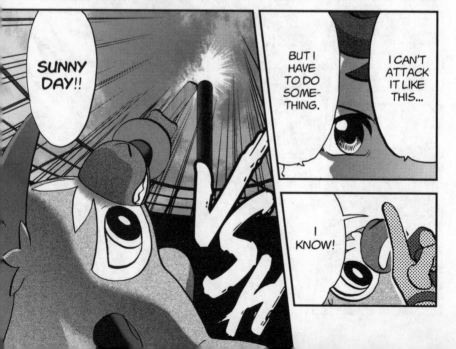

SUNNY DAY!!

BUT I HAVE TO DO SOME-THING.

I CAN'T ATTACK IT LIKE THIS...

I KNOW!

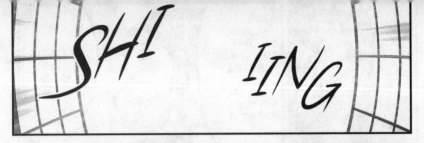

SHI IING

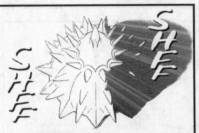

SHFF SHFF

SHFF SHFF

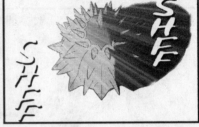

ACK!!

NOW!

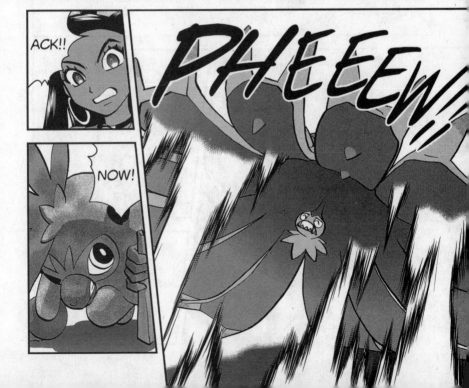

PHEEEW!!

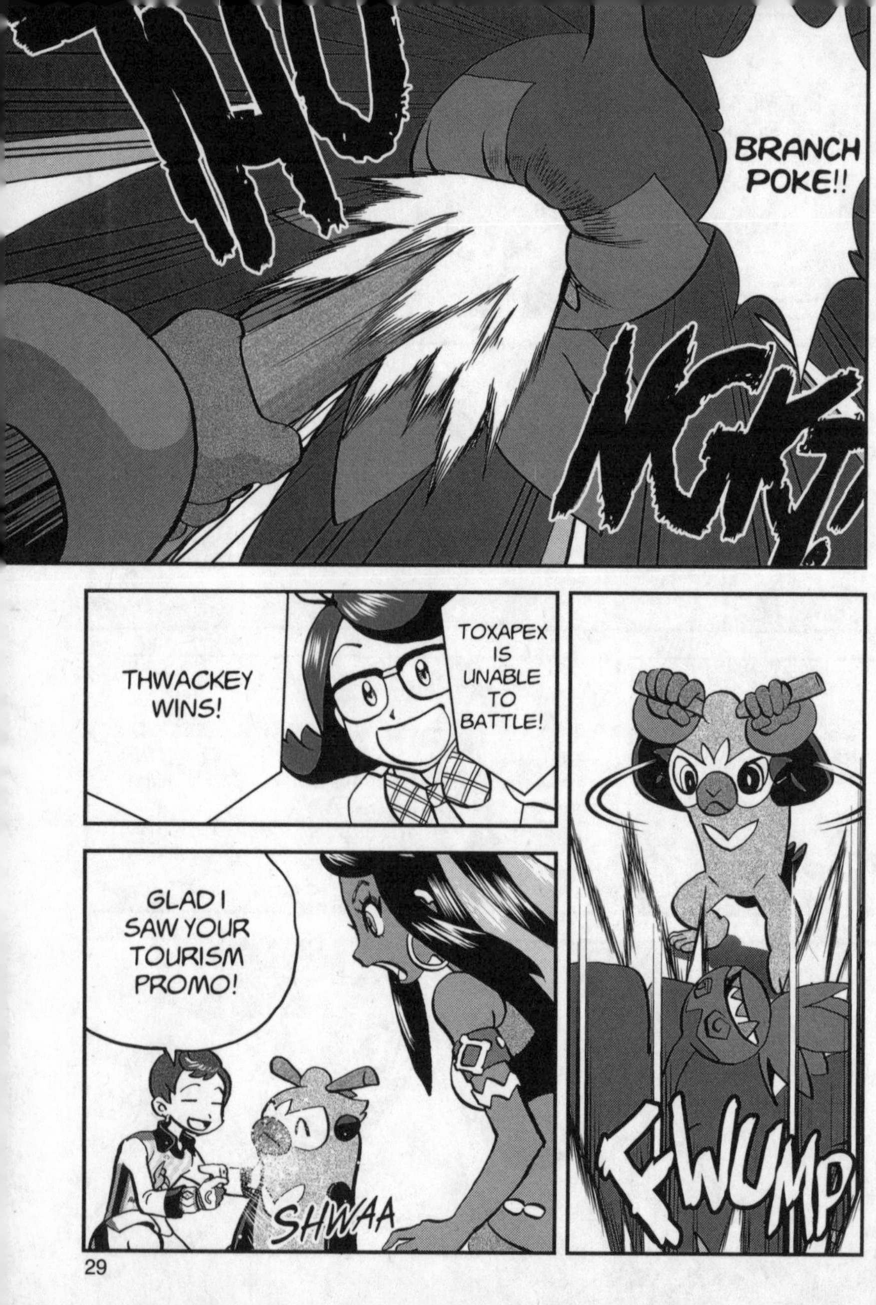
BRANCH POKE!!
THU
NGK!!
FWUMP
TOXAPEX IS UNABLE TO BATTLE!
THWACKEY WINS!
GLAD I SAW YOUR TOURISM PROMO!
SHWAA

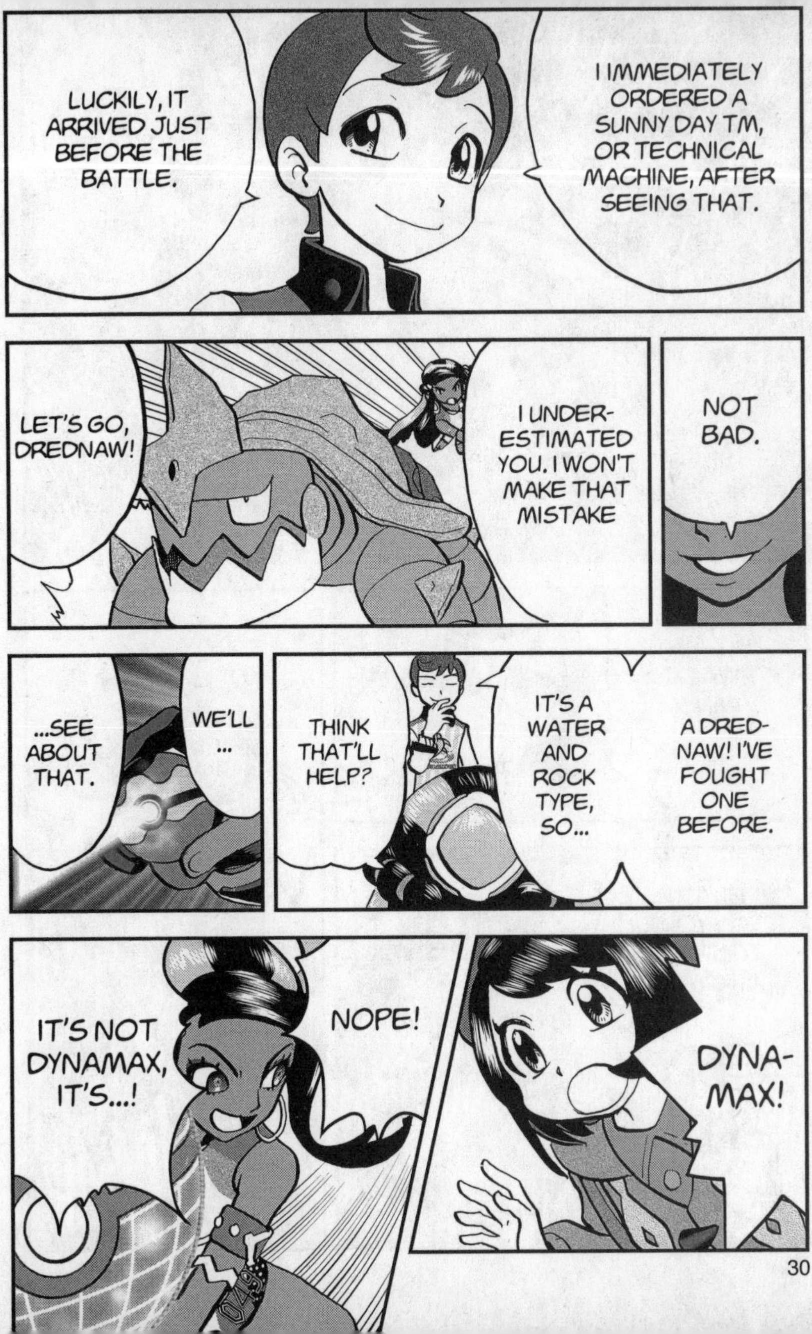
I IMMEDIATELY ORDERED A SUNNY DAY TM, OR TECHNICAL MACHINE, AFTER SEEING THAT.
LUCKILY, IT ARRIVED JUST BEFORE THE BATTLE.
NOT BAD.
I UNDER-ESTIMATED YOU. I WON'T MAKE THAT MISTAKE
LET'S GO, DREDNAW!
A DRED-NAW! I'VE FOUGHT ONE BEFORE.
IT'S A WATER AND ROCK TYPE, SO...
THINK THAT'LL HELP?
WE'LL ...
...SEE ABOUT THAT.
DYNA-MAX!
NOPE!
IT'S NOT DYNAMAX, IT'S...!

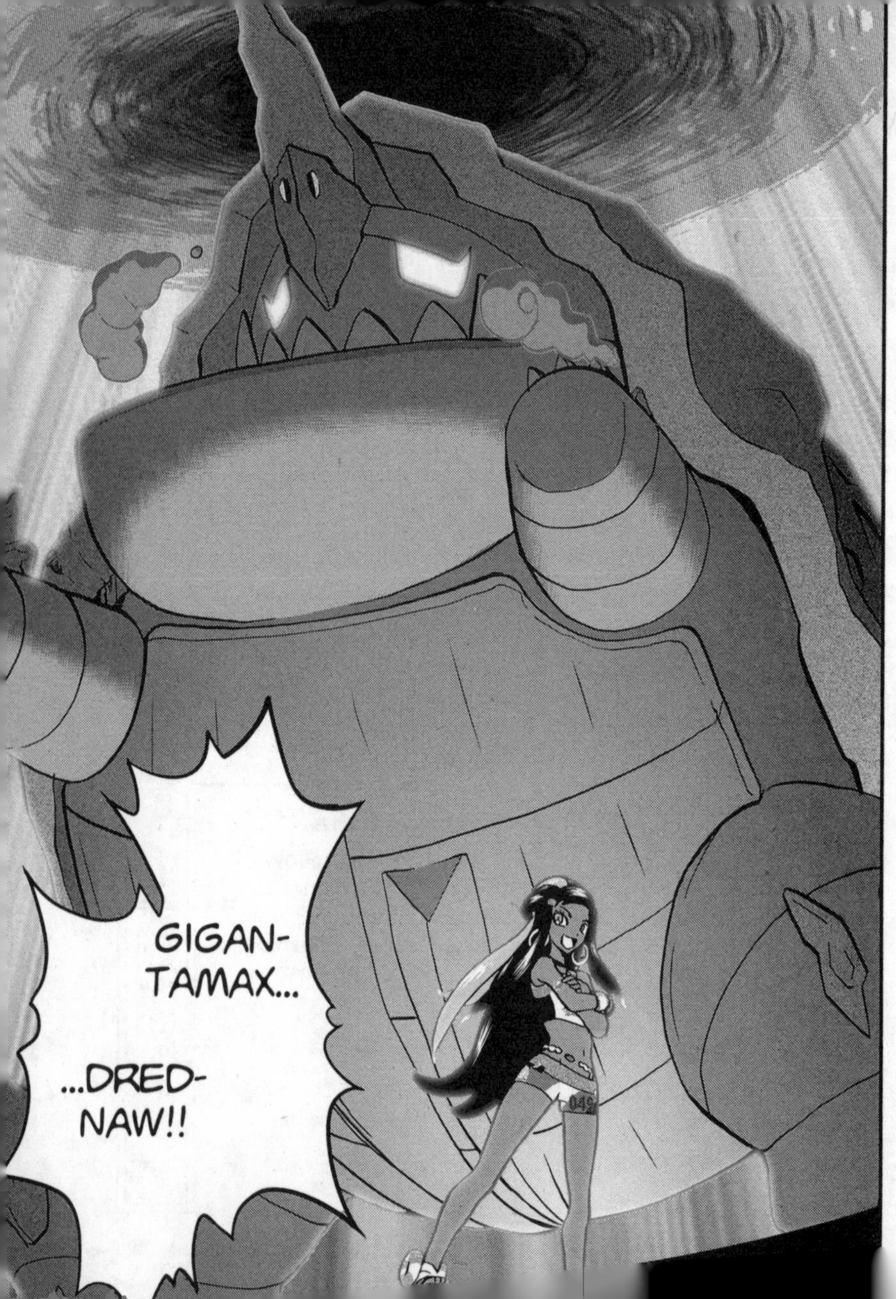
GIGAN-TAMAX...
...DRED-NAW!!

THE SECRETS OF DYNAMAX, PART 7

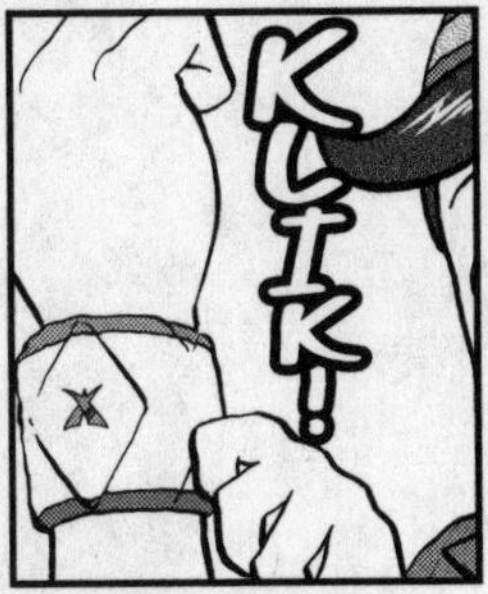
KLIK!

▲ Created by Professor Magnolia from Macro Cosmos technology

Dynamax Band

A wristband that allows a Trainer to Dynamax their Pokémon. Originally created out of a Wishing Star, it holds immense power!

Adventure 9 Splish Splash!! Gigantamax Battle

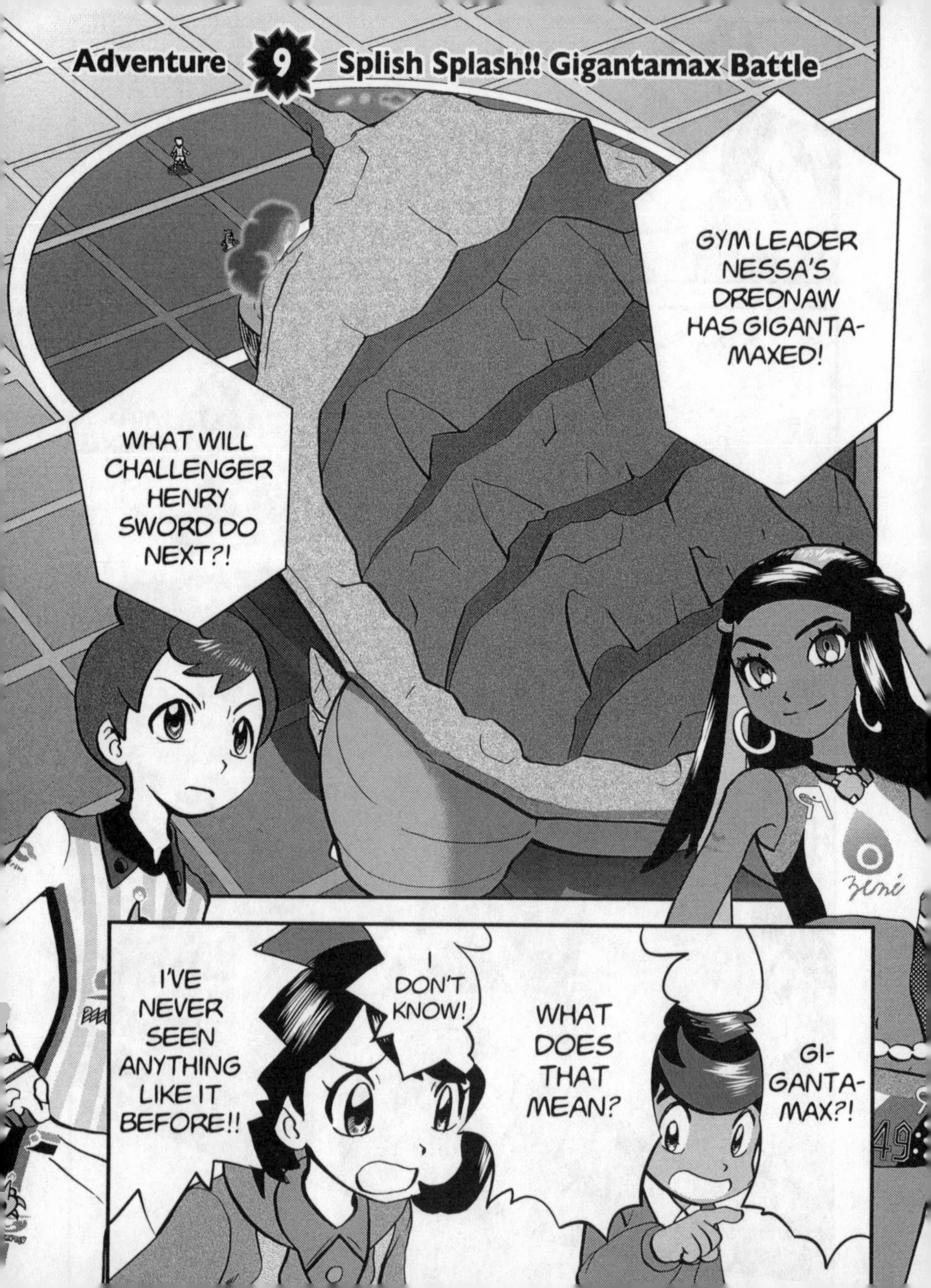
GYM LEADER NESSA'S DREDNAW HAS GIGANTA-MAXED!
WHAT WILL CHALLENGER HENRY SWORD DO NEXT?!
GI-GANTA-MAX?!
WHAT DOES THAT MEAN?
I DON'T KNOW!
I'VE NEVER SEEN ANYTHING LIKE IT BEFORE!!

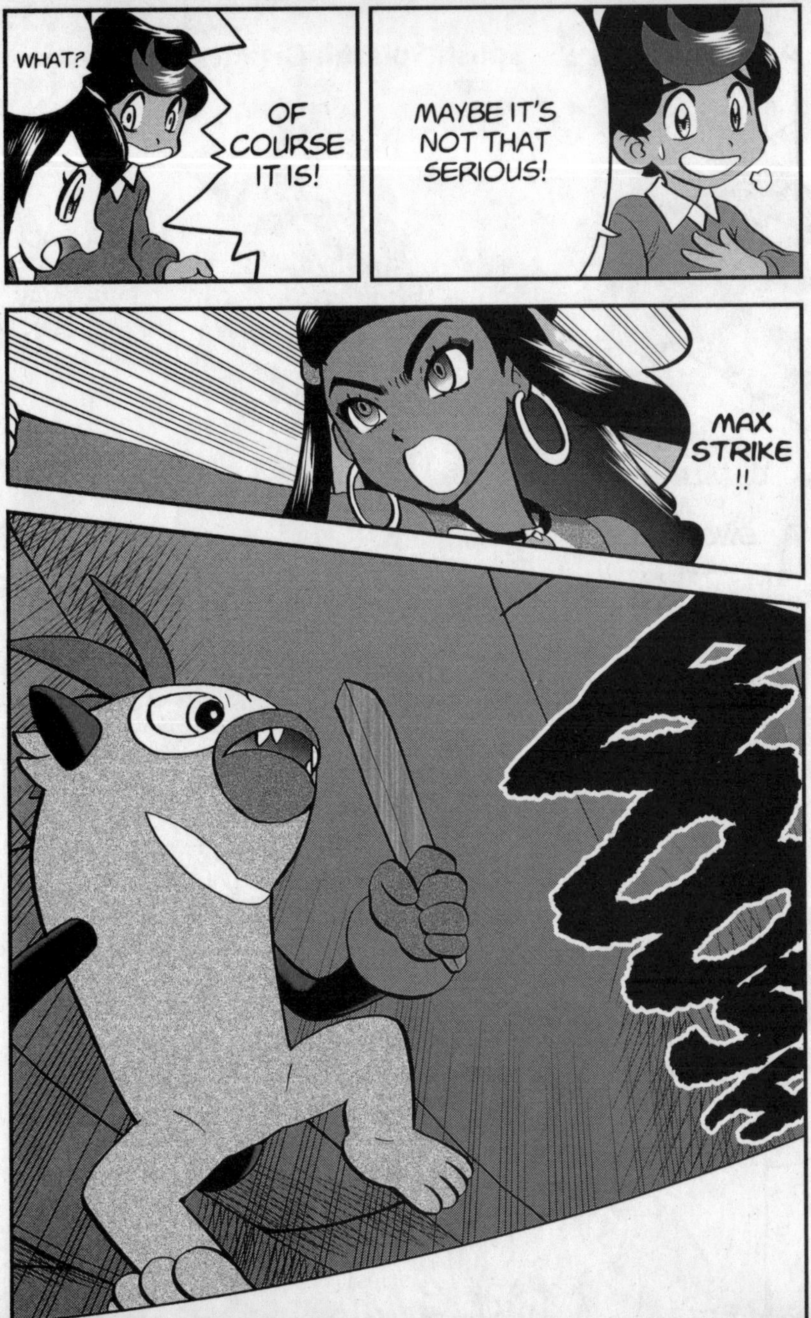
MAYBE IT'S NOT THAT SERIOUS!
WHAT?
OF COURSE IT IS!
MAX STRIKE !!

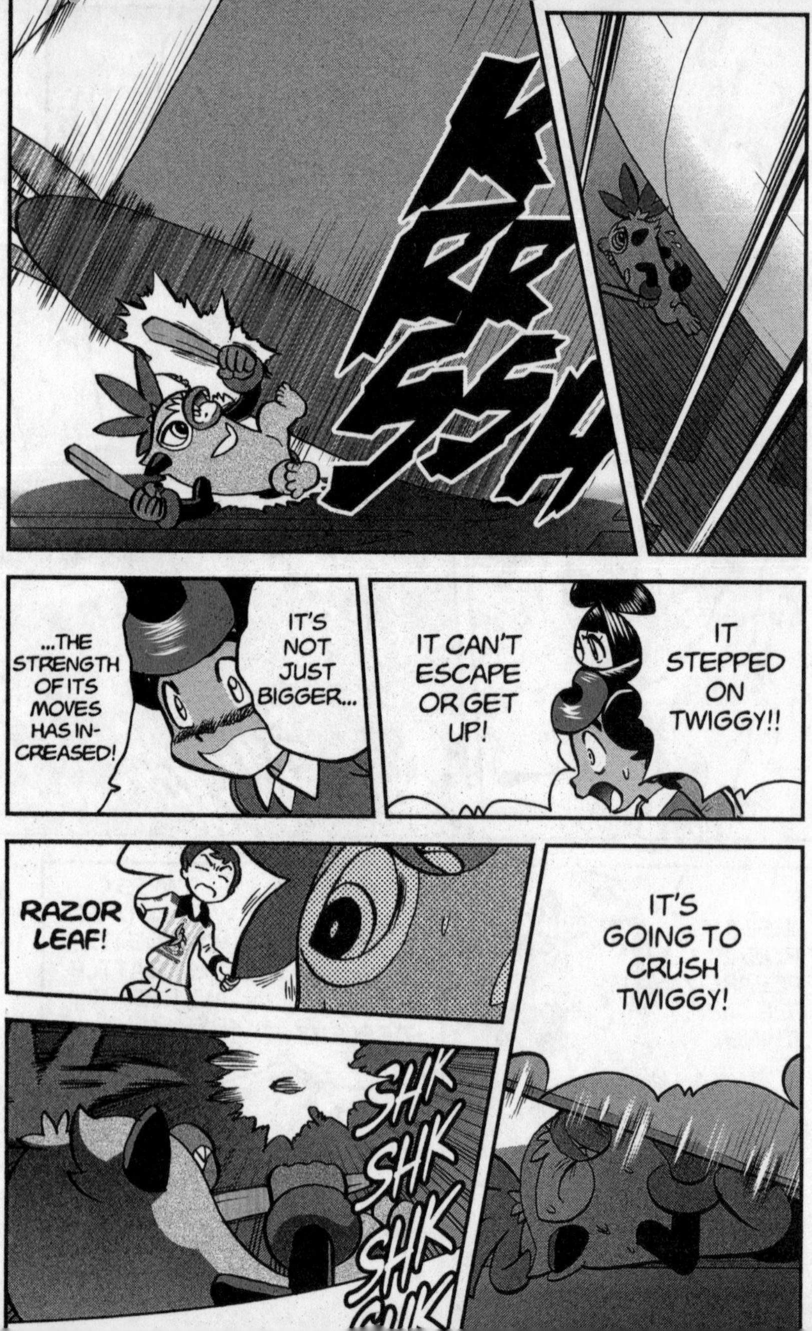

IT STEPPED ON TWIGGY!!
IT CAN'T ESCAPE OR GET UP!
IT'S NOT JUST BIGGER...
...THE STRENGTH OF ITS MOVES HAS INCREASED!
IT'S GOING TO CRUSH TWIGGY!
RAZOR LEAF!
SHK SHK SHK SHK

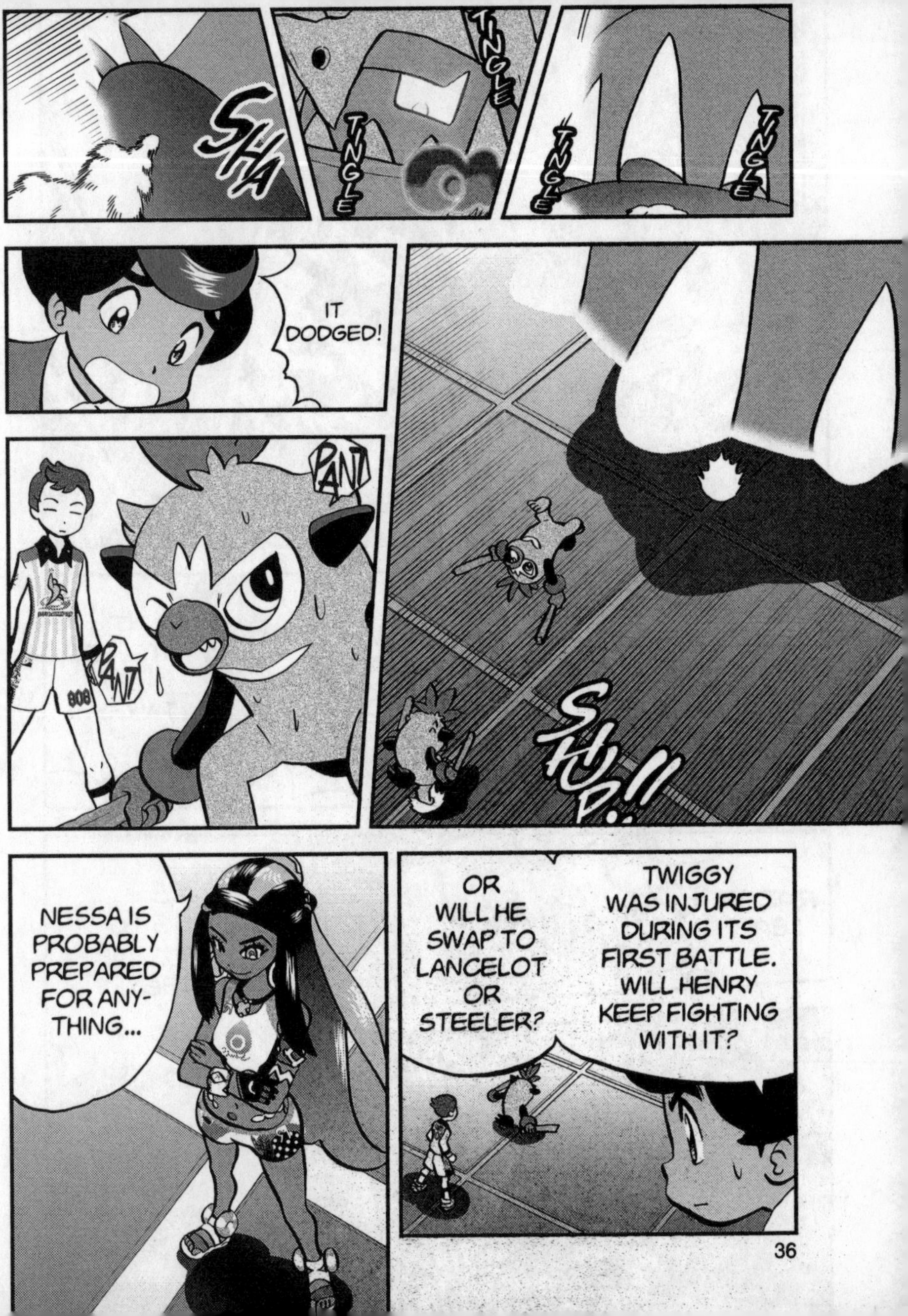
TINGLE
TINGLE
TINGLE
TINGLE
SHA
SHUP!!
IT DODGED!
PANT
PANT
TWIGGY WAS INJURED DURING ITS FIRST BATTLE. WILL HENRY KEEP FIGHTING WITH IT?
OR WILL HE SWAP TO LANCELOT OR STEELER?
NESSA IS PROBABLY PREPARED FOR ANY-THING...

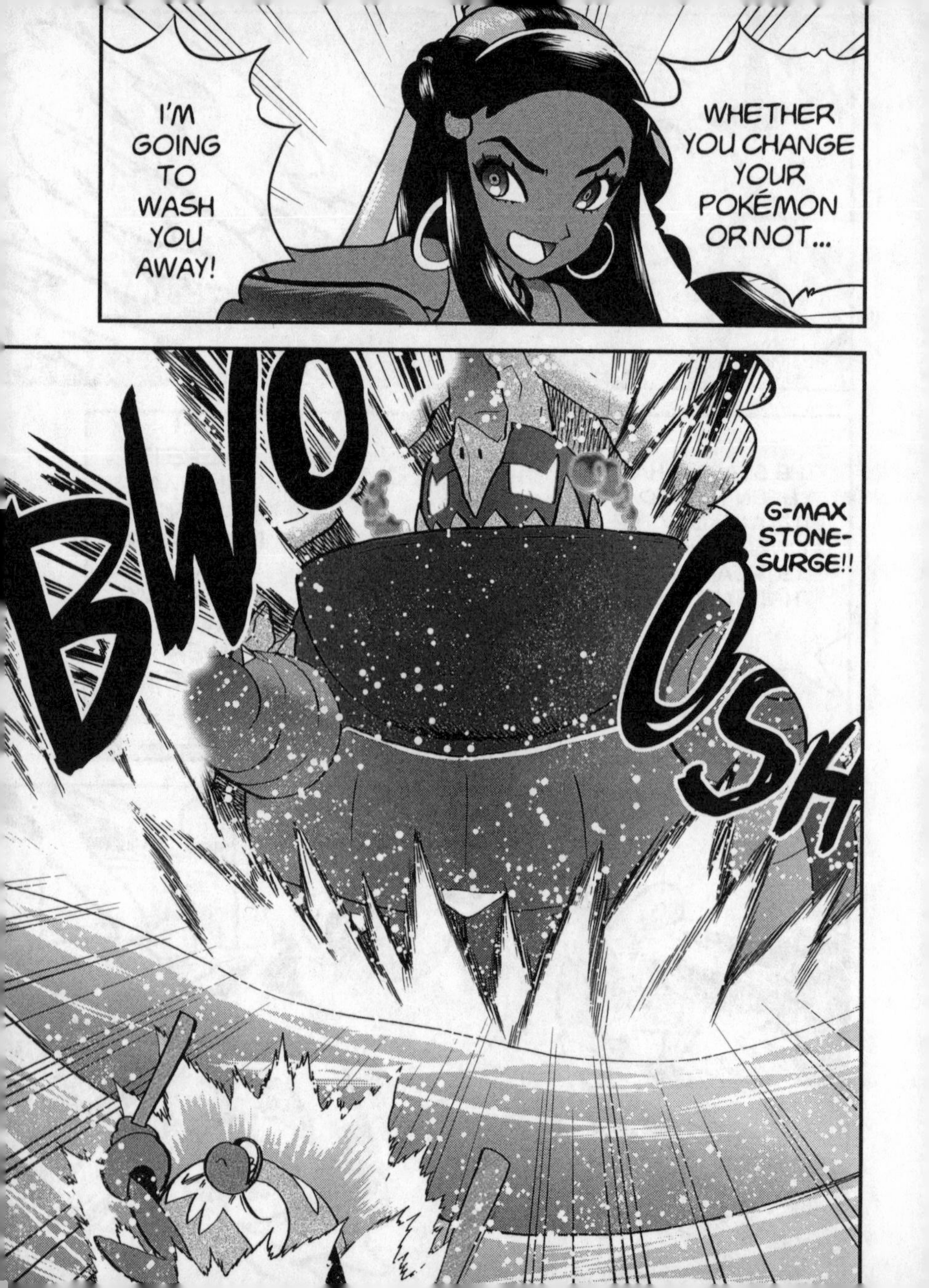
WHETHER YOU CHANGE YOUR POKÉMON OR NOT...
I'M GOING TO WASH YOU AWAY!
G-MAX STONE-SURGE!!
BWOOSH

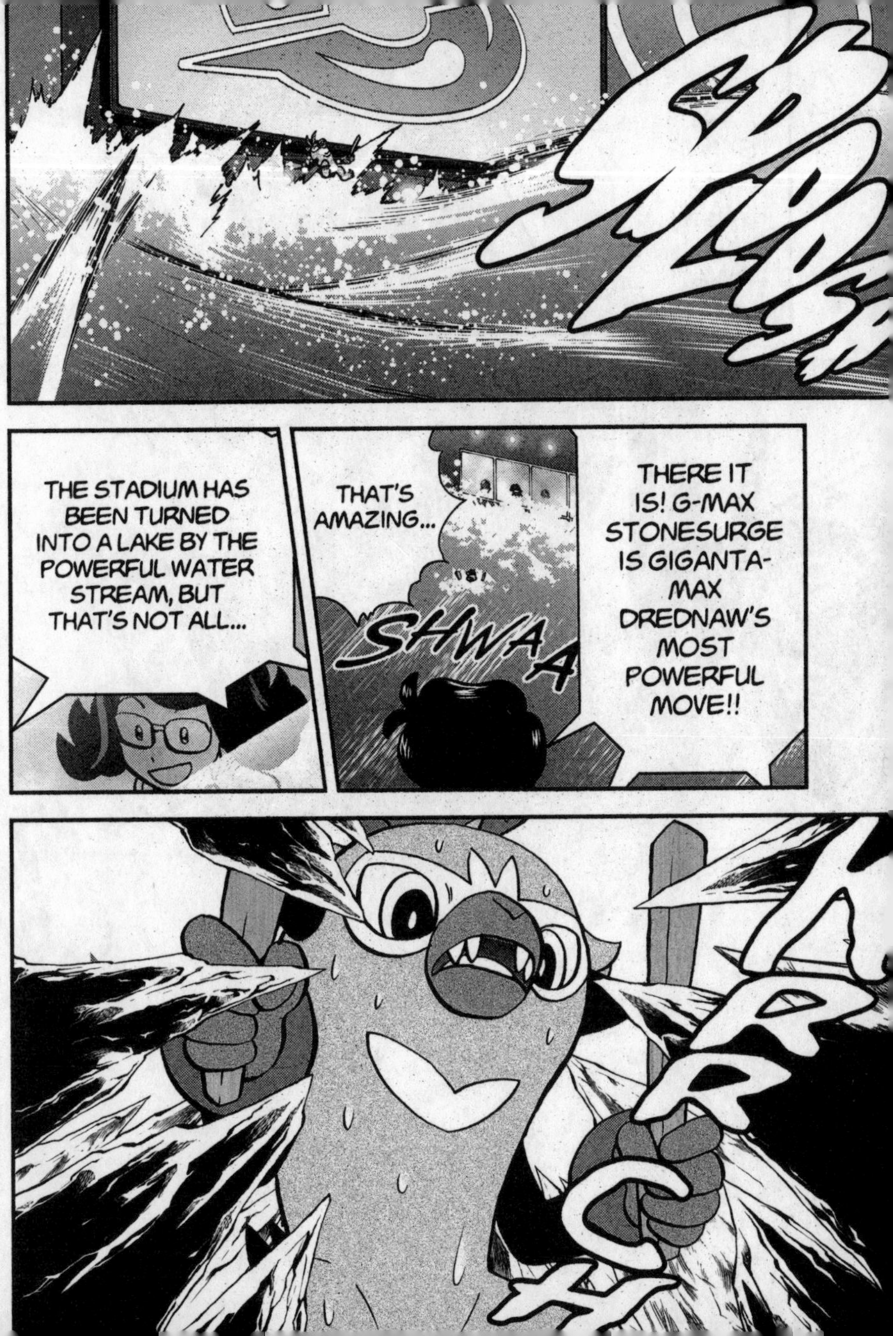
THERE IT IS! G-MAX STONESURGE IS GIGANTA-MAX DREDNAW'S MOST POWERFUL MOVE!!
THAT'S AMAZING...
SHWAA
THE STADIUM HAS BEEN TURNED INTO A LAKE BY THE POWERFUL WATER STREAM, BUT THAT'S NOT ALL...

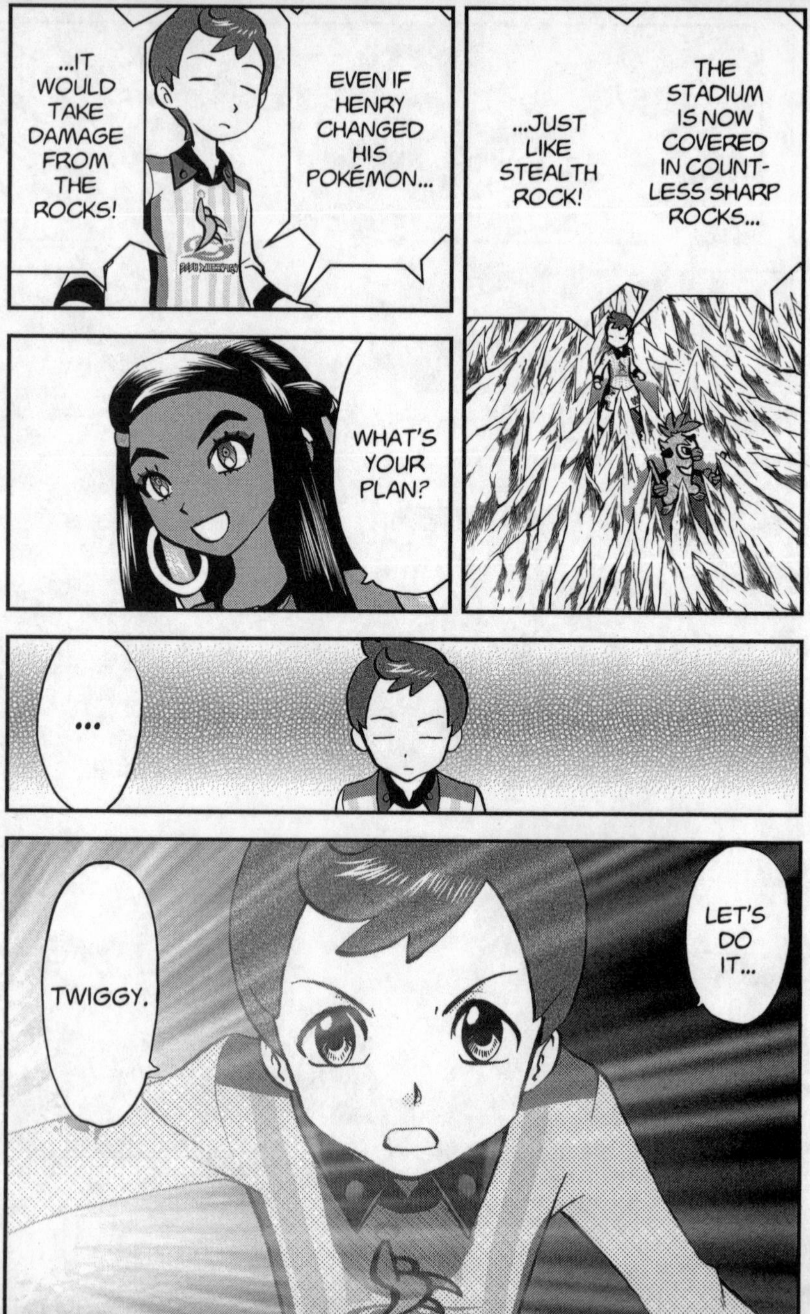
THE STADIUM IS NOW COVERED IN COUNTLESS SHARP ROCKS...
...JUST LIKE STEALTH ROCK!
EVEN IF HENRY CHANGED HIS POKÉMON...
...IT WOULD TAKE DAMAGE FROM THE ROCKS!
WHAT'S YOUR PLAN?
...
LET'S DO IT...
TWIGGY.

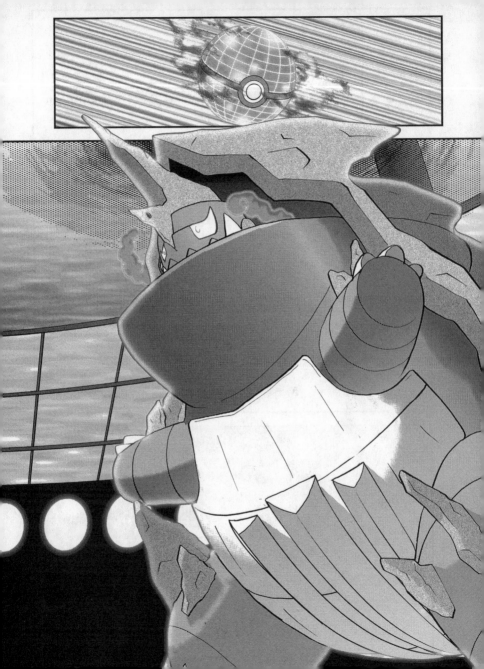

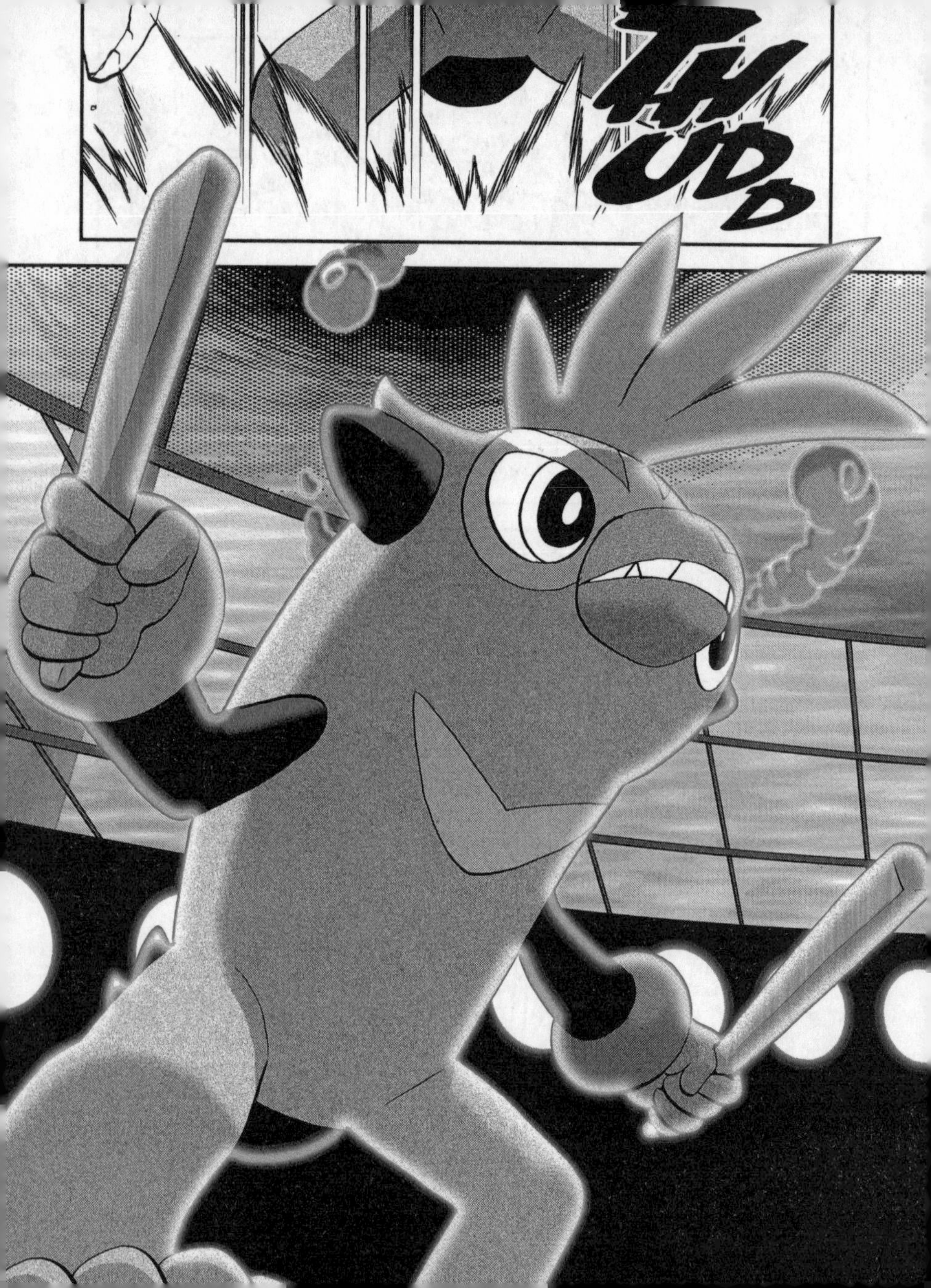
THUDD

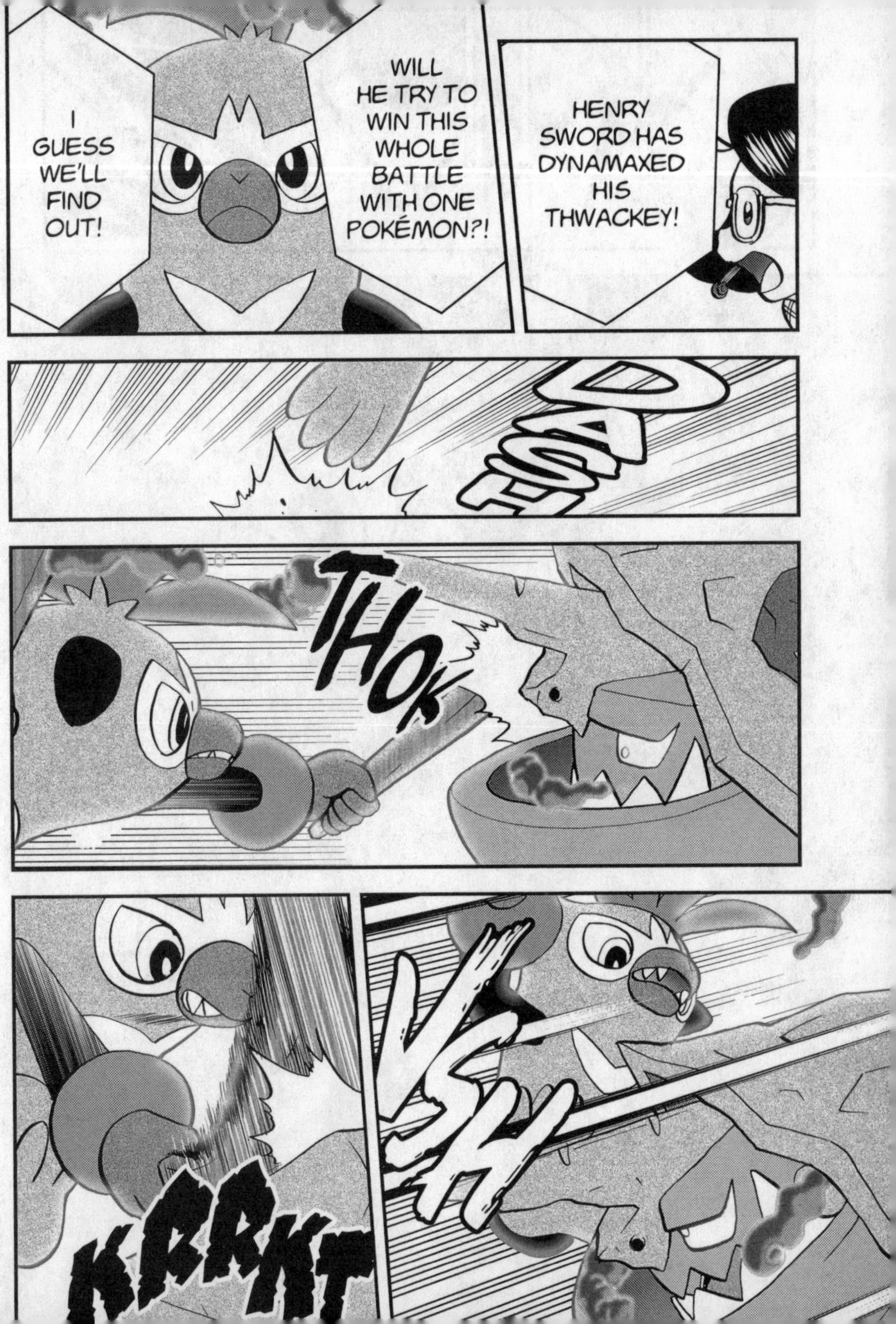

HENRY SWORD HAS DYNAMAXED HIS THWACKEY!
WILL HE TRY TO WIN THIS WHOLE BATTLE WITH ONE POKÉMON?!
I GUESS WE'LL FIND OUT!
DASH
THOK
VSH
KRRKT

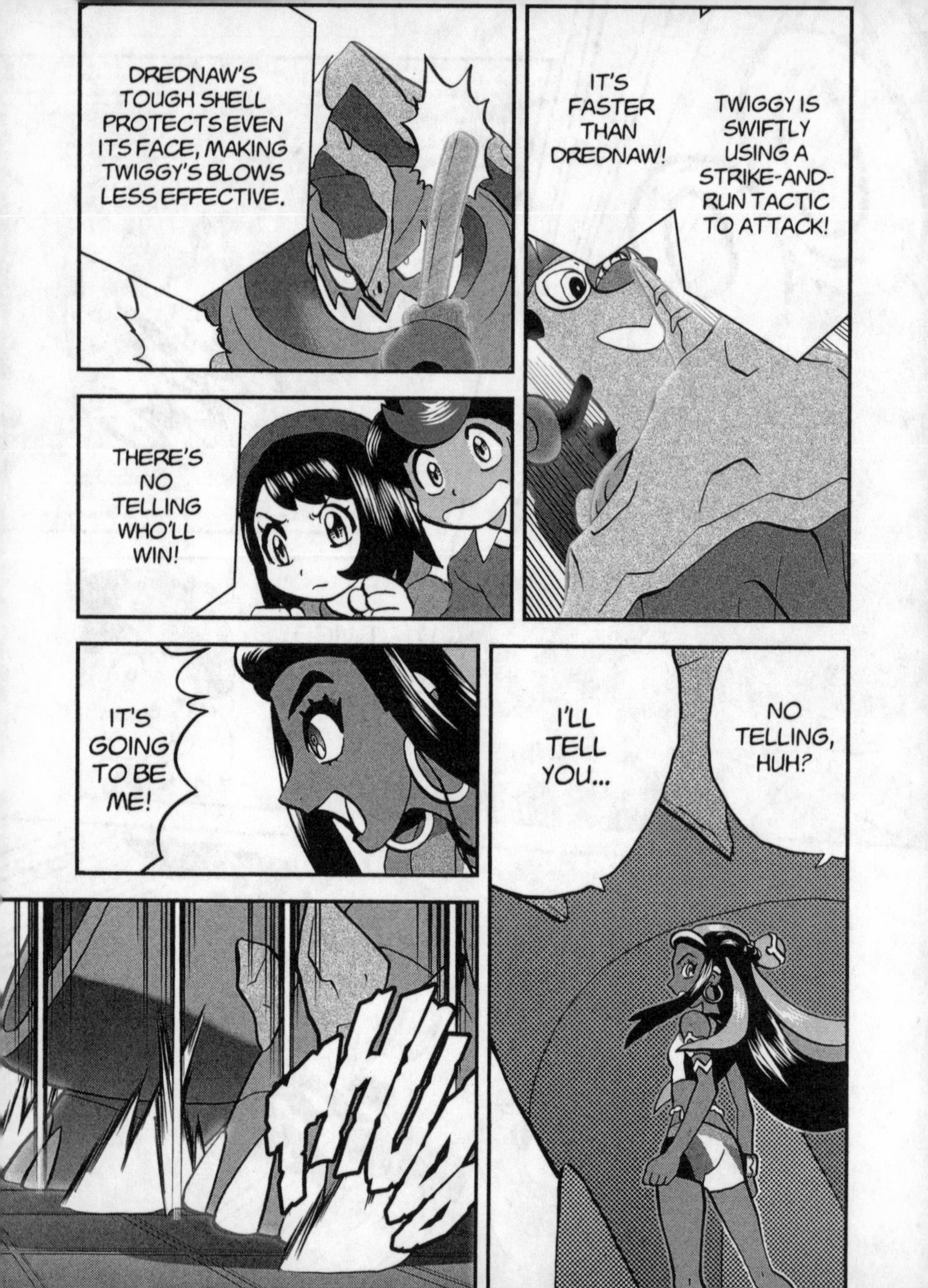
TWIGGY IS SWIFTLY USING A STRIKE-AND-RUN TACTIC TO ATTACK!
IT'S FASTER THAN DREDNAW!
DREDNAW'S TOUGH SHELL PROTECTS EVEN ITS FACE, MAKING TWIGGY'S BLOWS LESS EFFECTIVE.
THERE'S NO TELLING WHO'LL WIN!
NO TELLING, HUH?
I'LL TELL YOU...
IT'S GOING TO BE ME!
THUD

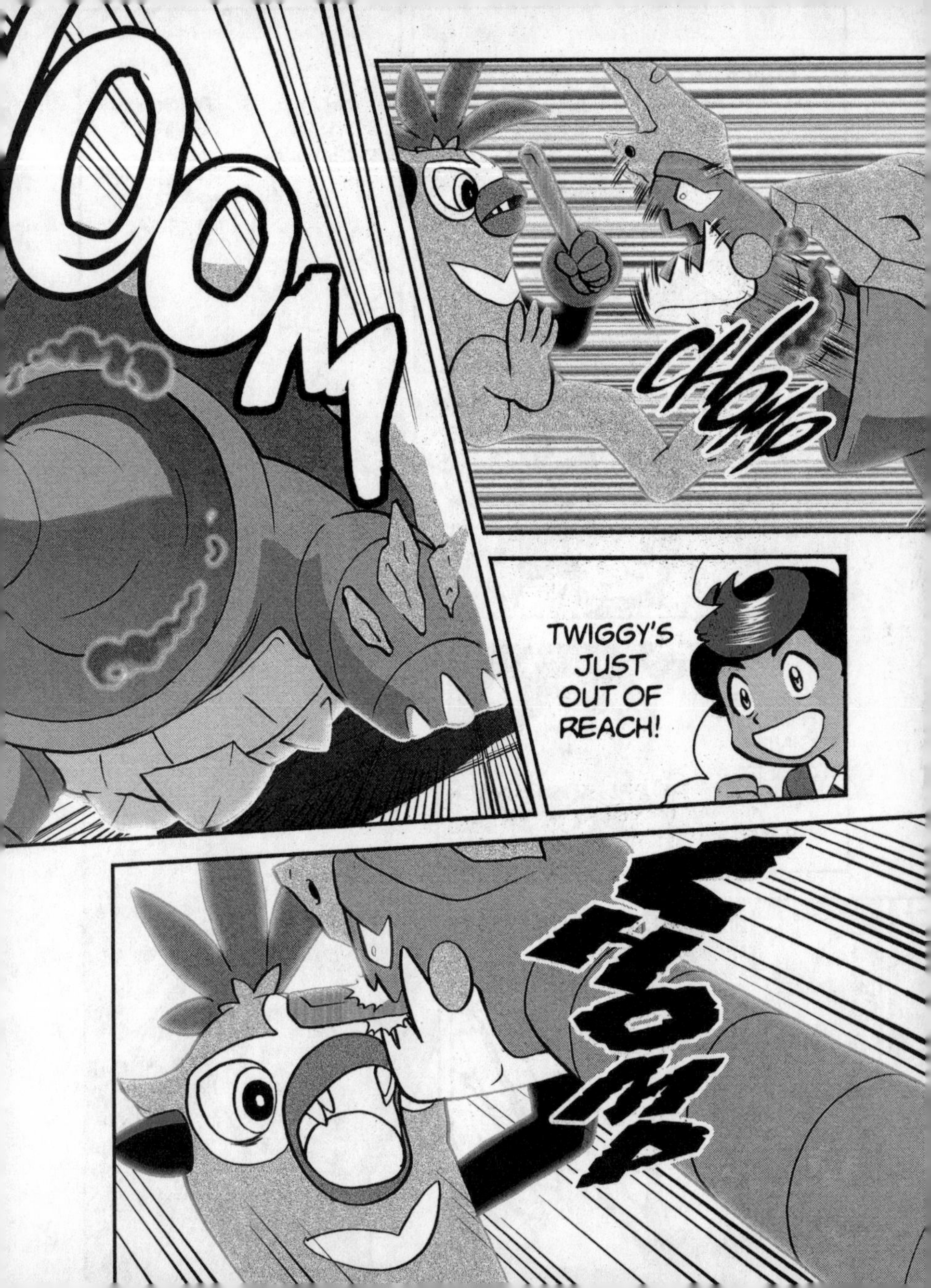
CHOMP
TWIGGY'S JUST OUT OF REACH!
OOOM
STOMP

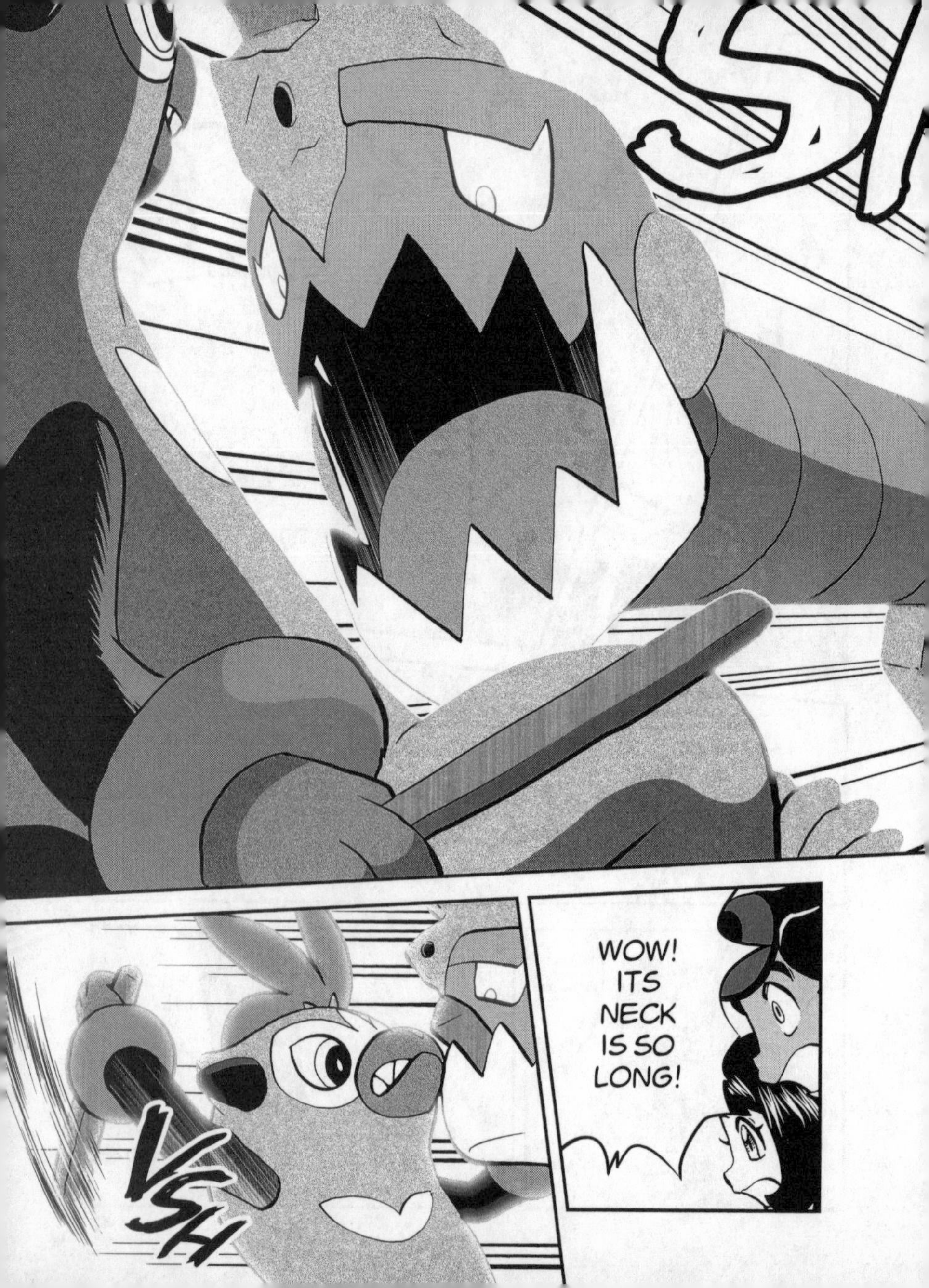
WOW! ITS NECK IS SO LONG!
VSH

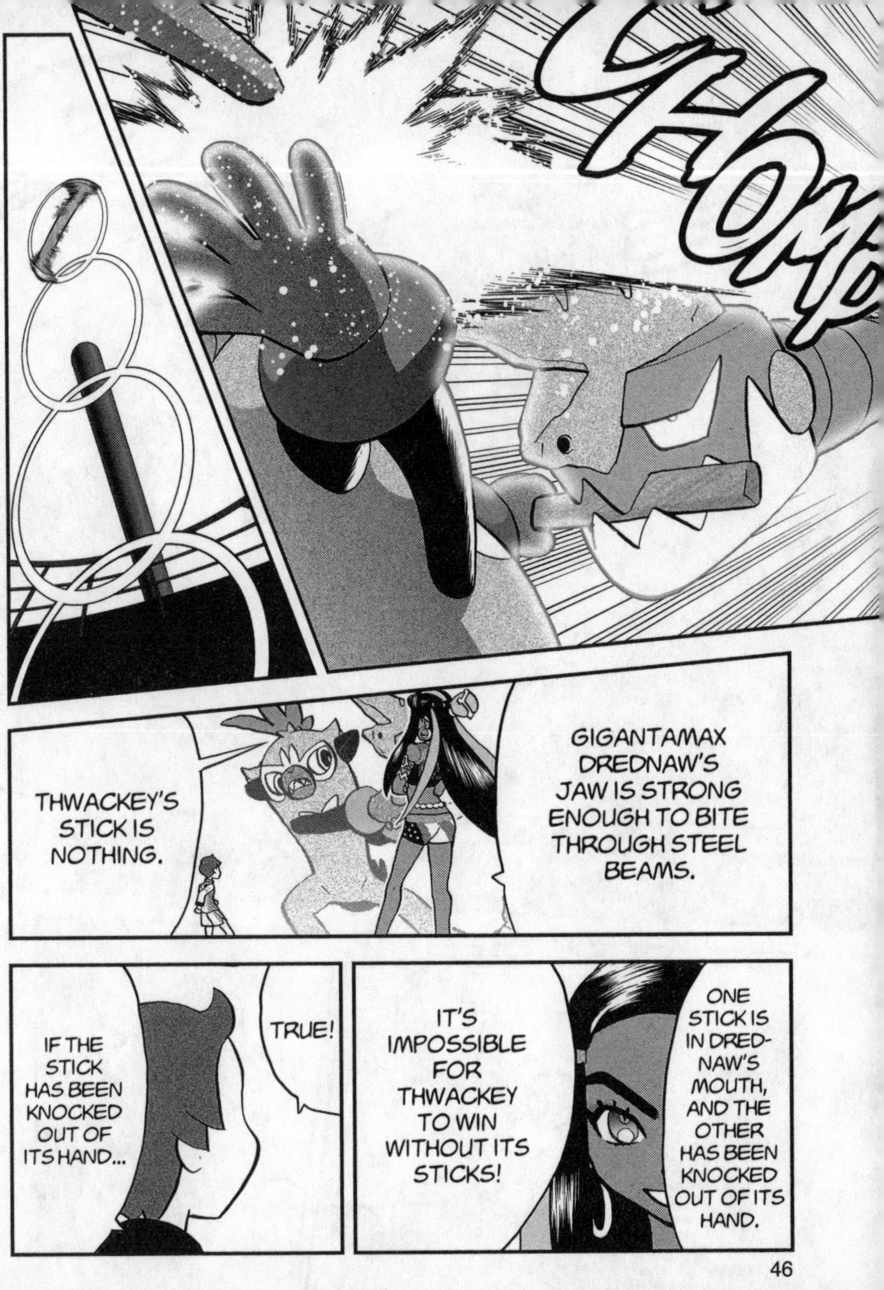
CHOMP
GIGANTAMAX DREDNAW'S JAW IS STRONG ENOUGH TO BITE THROUGH STEEL BEAMS.
THWACKEY'S STICK IS NOTHING.
ONE STICK IS IN DRED-NAW'S MOUTH, AND THE OTHER HAS BEEN KNOCKED OUT OF ITS HAND.
IT'S IMPOSSIBLE FOR THWACKEY TO WIN WITHOUT ITS STICKS!
TRUE!
IF THE STICK HAS BEEN KNOCKED OUT OF ITS HAND...

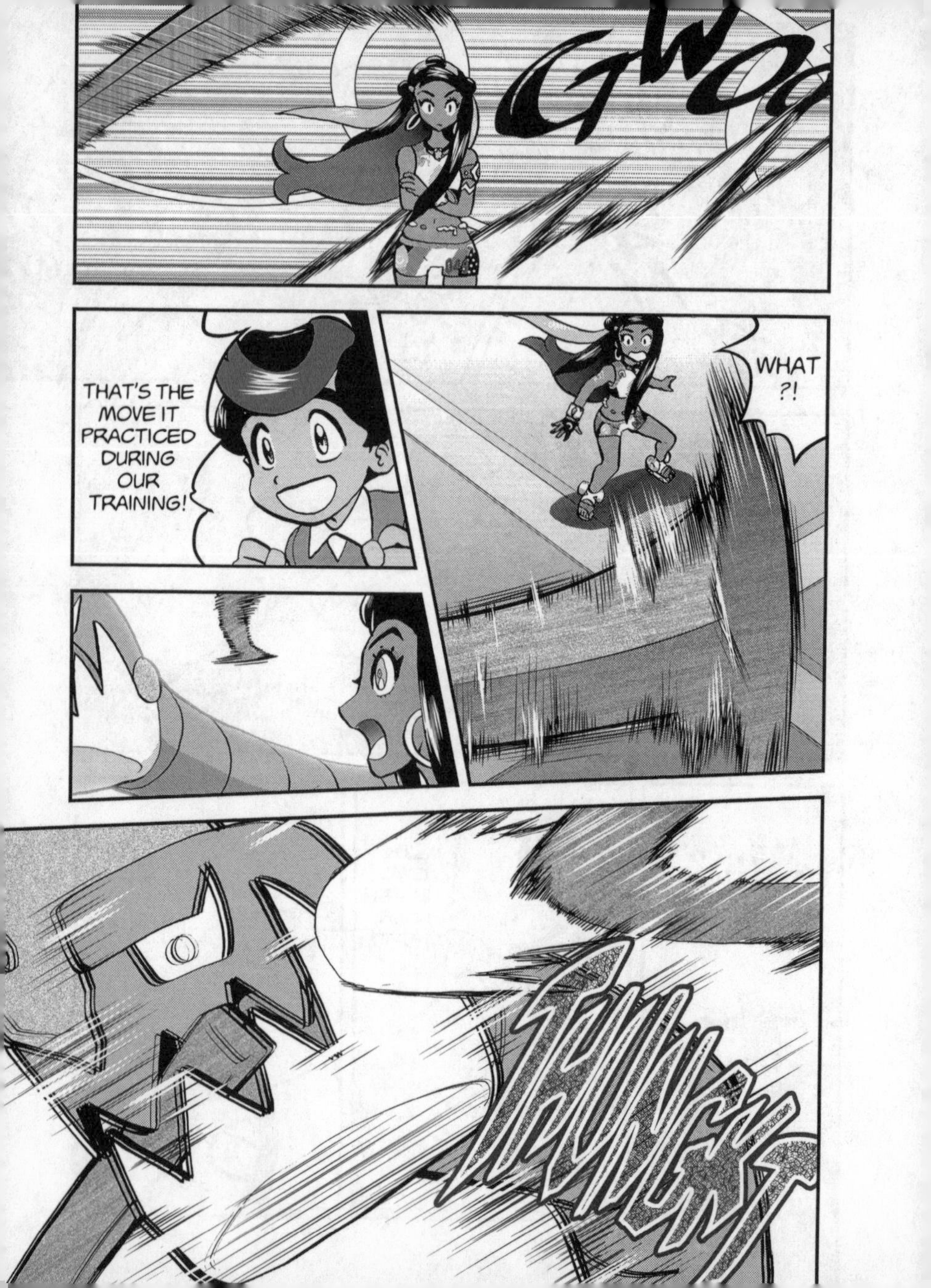
WHAT ?!
THAT'S THE MOVE IT PRACTICED DURING OUR TRAINING!

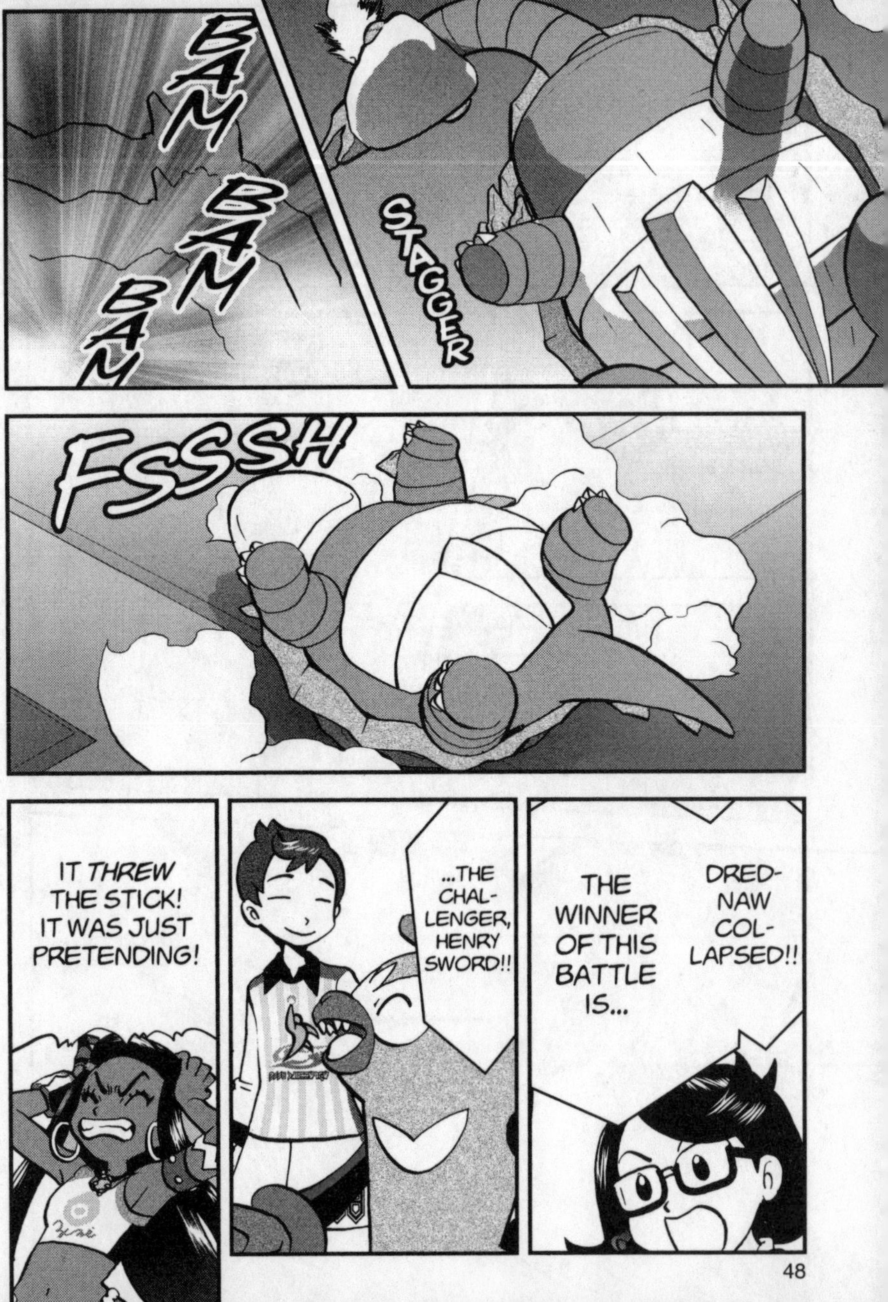
STAGGER
BAM BAM BAM
FSSSH
DRED-NAW COL-LAPSED!!
THE WINNER OF THIS BATTLE IS...
...THE CHAL-LENGER, HENRY SWORD!!
IT THREW THE STICK! IT WAS JUST PRETENDING!

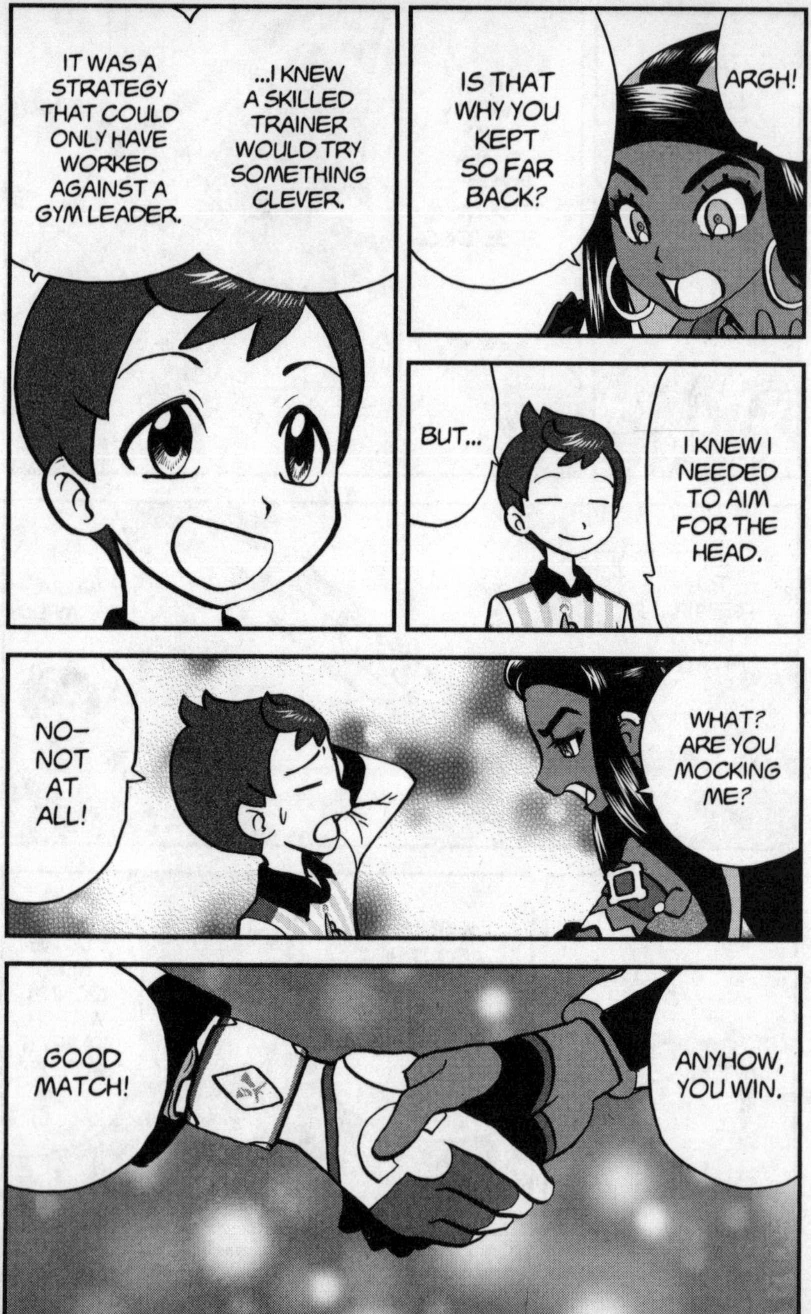
ARGH!
IS THAT WHY YOU KEPT SO FAR BACK?
BUT...
I KNEW I NEEDED TO AIM FOR THE HEAD.
...I KNEW A SKILLED TRAINER WOULD TRY SOMETHING CLEVER.
IT WAS A STRATEGY THAT COULD ONLY HAVE WORKED AGAINST A GYM LEADER.
WHAT? ARE YOU MOCKING ME?
NO—NOT AT ALL!
ANYHOW, YOU WIN.
GOOD MATCH!

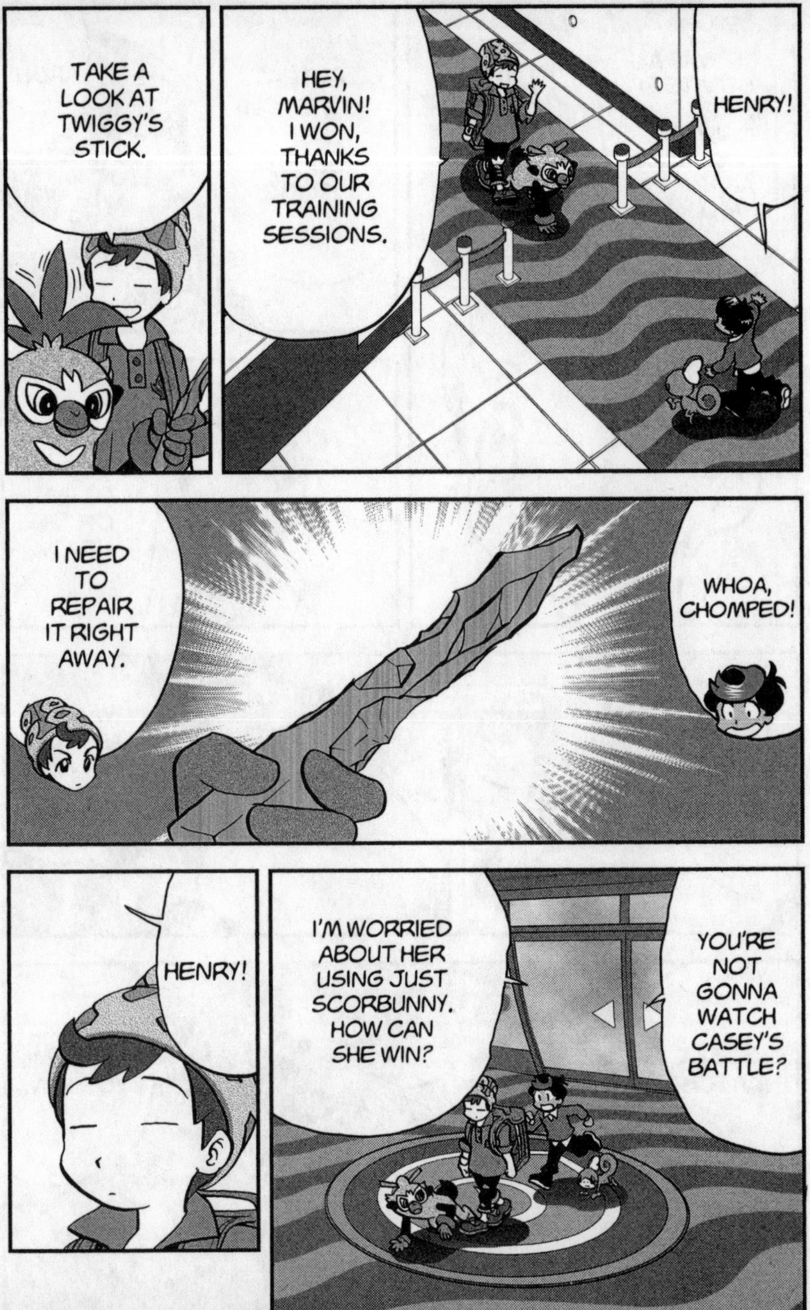
HENRY!
HEY, MARVIN! I WON, THANKS TO OUR TRAINING SESSIONS.
TAKE A LOOK AT TWIGGY'S STICK.
WHOA, CHOMPED!
I NEED TO REPAIR IT RIGHT AWAY.
YOU'RE NOT GONNA WATCH CASEY'S BATTLE?
I'M WORRIED ABOUT HER USING JUST SCORBUNNY. HOW CAN SHE WIN?
HENRY!

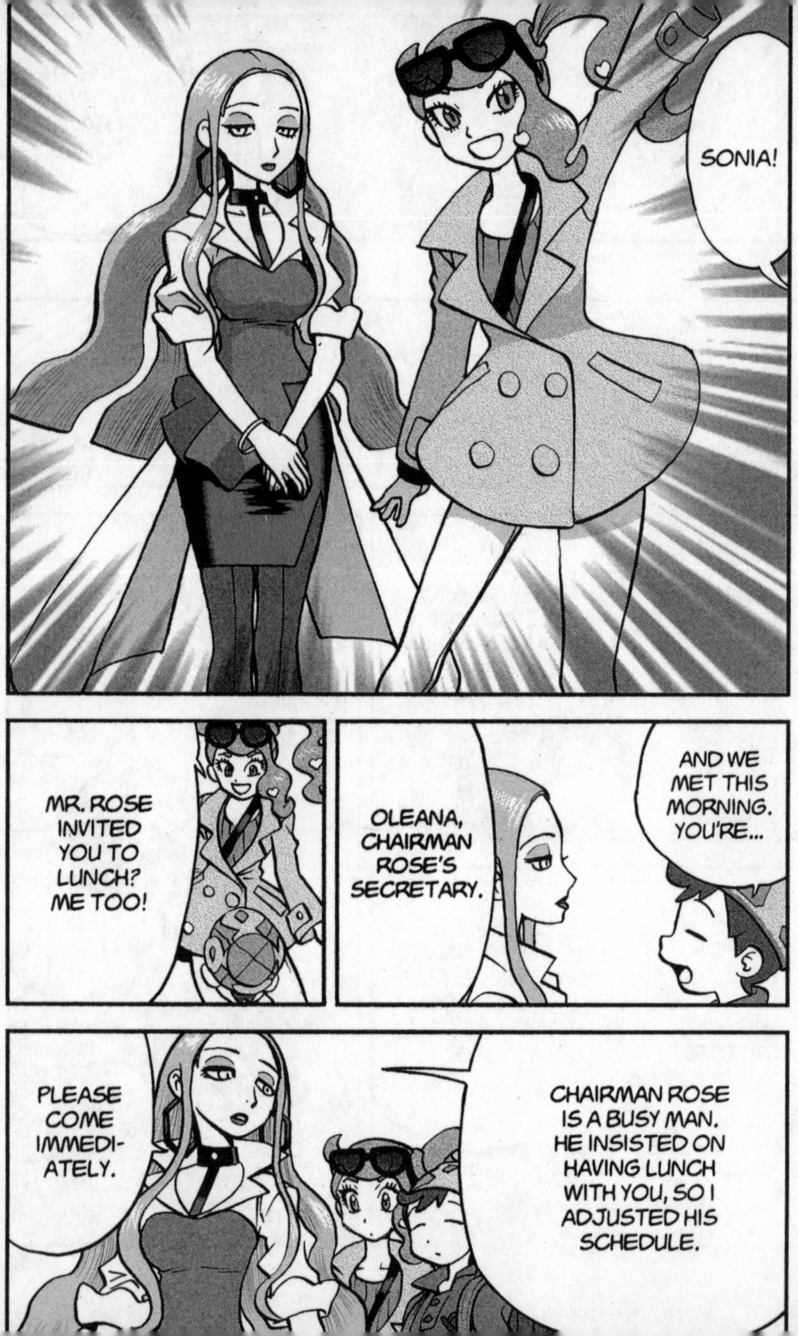
SONIA!
AND WE MET THIS MORNING. YOU'RE...
OLEANA, CHAIRMAN ROSE'S SECRETARY.
MR. ROSE INVITED YOU TO LUNCH? ME TOO!
CHAIRMAN ROSE IS A BUSY MAN. HE INSISTED ON HAVING LUNCH WITH YOU, SO I ADJUSTED HIS SCHEDULE.
PLEASE COME IMMEDI-ATELY.

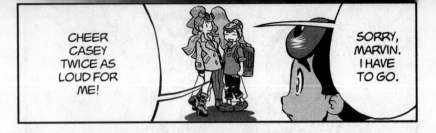

CHEER CASEY TWICE AS LOUD FOR ME!

SORRY, MARVIN. I HAVE TO GO.

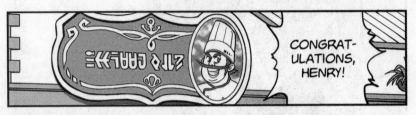

CONGRAT-ULATIONS, HENRY!

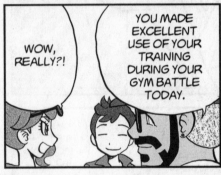

WOW, REALLY?!

YOU MADE EXCELLENT USE OF YOUR TRAINING DURING YOUR GYM BATTLE TODAY.

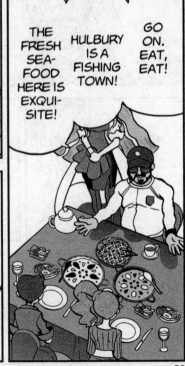

THE FRESH SEA-FOOD HERE IS EXQUI-SITE!

HULBURY IS A FISHING TOWN!

GO ON. EAT, EAT!

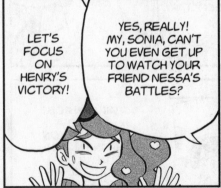

LET'S FOCUS ON HENRY'S VICTORY!

YES, REALLY! MY, SONIA, CAN'T YOU EVEN GET UP TO WATCH YOUR FRIEND NESSA'S BATTLES?

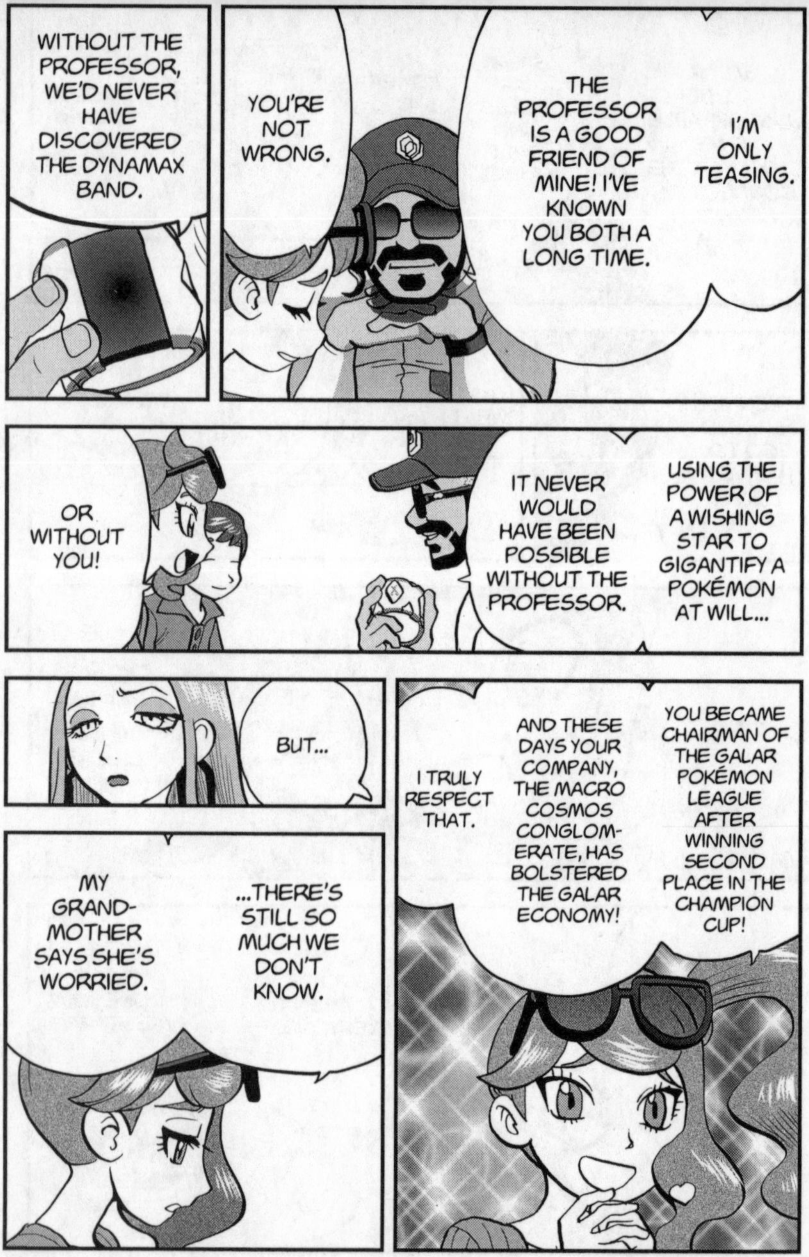
I'M ONLY TEASING.
THE PROFESSOR IS A GOOD FRIEND OF MINE! I'VE KNOWN YOU BOTH A LONG TIME.
YOU'RE NOT WRONG.
WITHOUT THE PROFESSOR, WE'D NEVER HAVE DISCOVERED THE DYNAMAX BAND.
USING THE POWER OF A WISHING STAR TO GIGANTIFY A POKÉMON AT WILL...
IT NEVER WOULD HAVE BEEN POSSIBLE WITHOUT THE PROFESSOR.
OR WITHOUT YOU!
YOU BECAME CHAIRMAN OF THE GALAR POKÉMON LEAGUE AFTER WINNING SECOND PLACE IN THE CHAMPION CUP!
AND THESE DAYS YOUR COMPANY, THE MACRO COSMOS CONGLOM-ERATE, HAS BOLSTERED THE GALAR ECONOMY!
I TRULY RESPECT THAT.
BUT...
...THERE'S STILL SO MUCH WE DON'T KNOW.
MY GRAND-MOTHER SAYS SHE'S WORRIED.

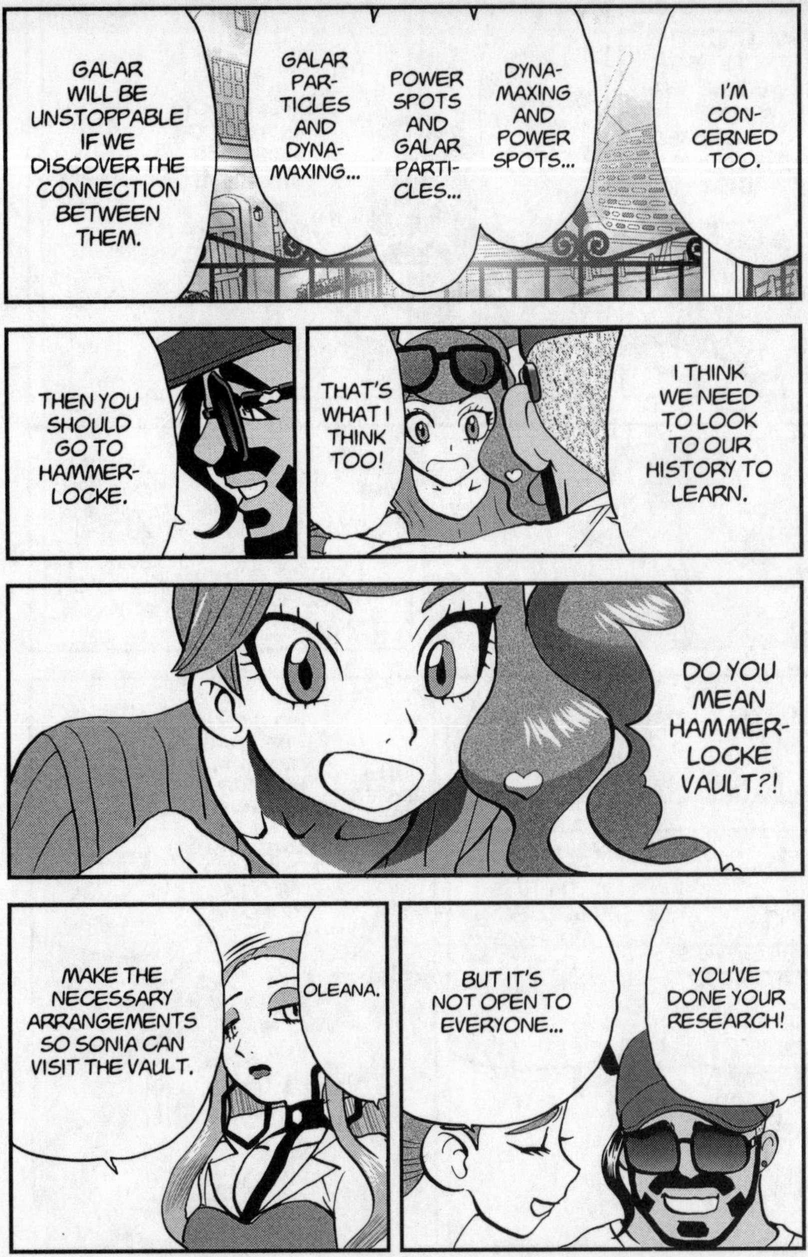
I'M CONCERNED TOO.
DYNAMAXING AND POWER SPOTS...
POWER SPOTS AND GALAR PARTICLES...
GALAR PARTICLES AND DYNAMAXING...
GALAR WILL BE UNSTOPPABLE IF WE DISCOVER THE CONNECTION BETWEEN THEM.
I THINK WE NEED TO LOOK TO OUR HISTORY TO LEARN.
THAT'S WHAT I THINK TOO!
THEN YOU SHOULD GO TO HAMMERLOCKE.
DO YOU MEAN HAMMERLOCKE VAULT?!
YOU'VE DONE YOUR RESEARCH!
BUT IT'S NOT OPEN TO EVERYONE...
OLEANA.
MAKE THE NECESSARY ARRANGEMENTS SO SONIA CAN VISIT THE VAULT.

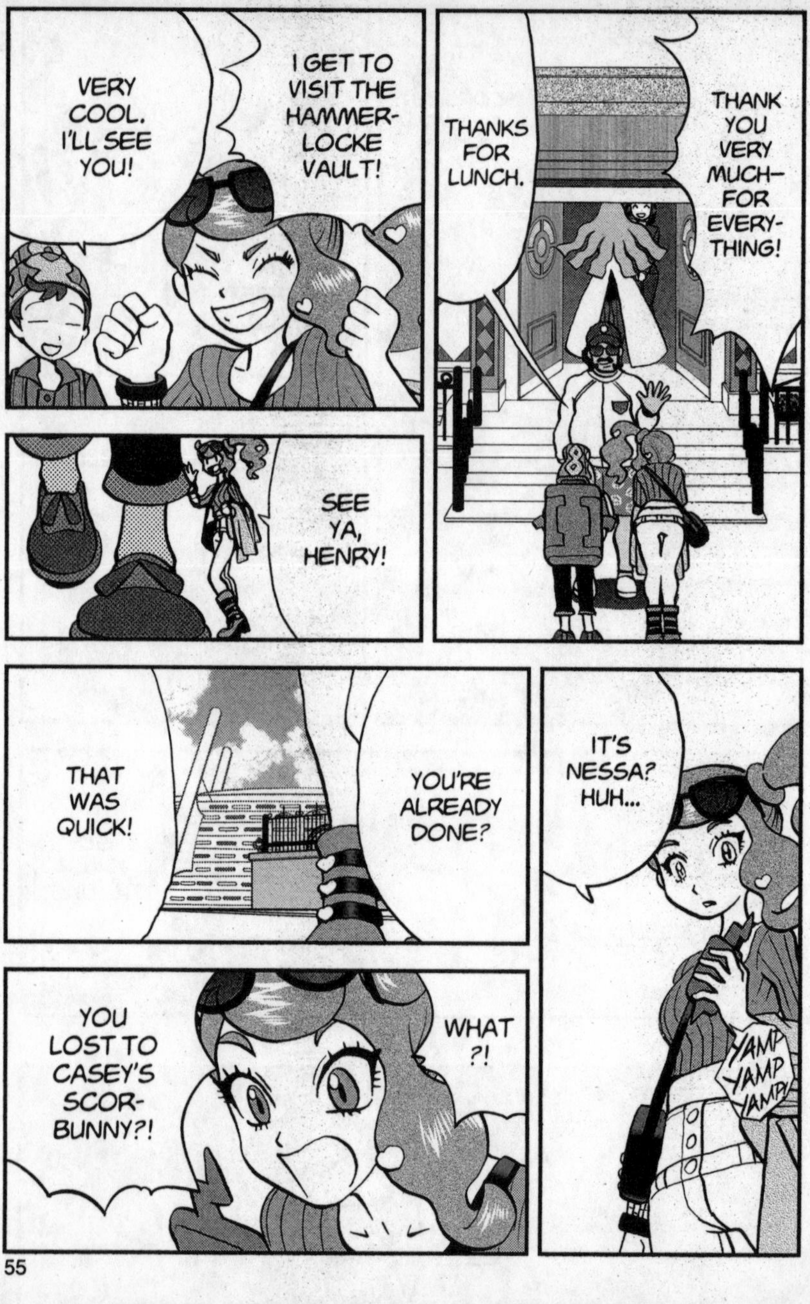
THANK YOU VERY MUCH—FOR EVERYTHING!
THANKS FOR LUNCH.
I GET TO VISIT THE HAMMER-LOCKE VAULT!
VERY COOL. I'LL SEE YOU!
SEE YA, HENRY!
IT'S NESSA? HUH...
YAMP YAMP YAMP!
YOU'RE ALREADY DONE?
THAT WAS QUICK!
WHAT?!
YOU LOST TO CASEY'S SCOR-BUNNY?!

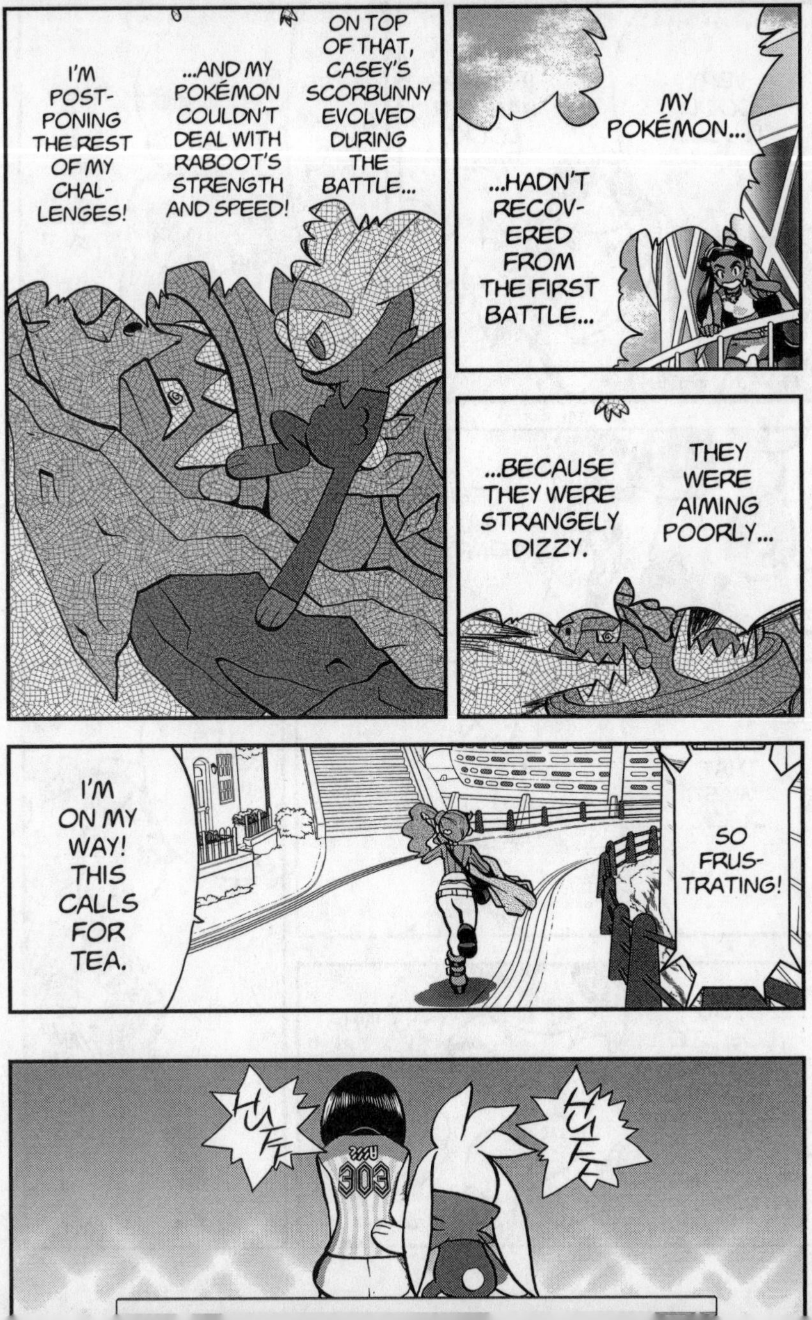
MY POKÉMON...
...HADN'T RECOVERED FROM THE FIRST BATTLE...
THEY WERE AIMING POORLY...
...BECAUSE THEY WERE STRANGELY DIZZY.
ON TOP OF THAT, CASEY'S SCORBUNNY EVOLVED DURING THE BATTLE...
...AND MY POKÉMON COULDN'T DEAL WITH RABOOT'S STRENGTH AND SPEED!
I'M POSTPONING THE REST OF MY CHALLENGES!
SO FRUSTRATING!
I'M ON MY WAY! THIS CALLS FOR TEA.
HUFF
HUFF
303

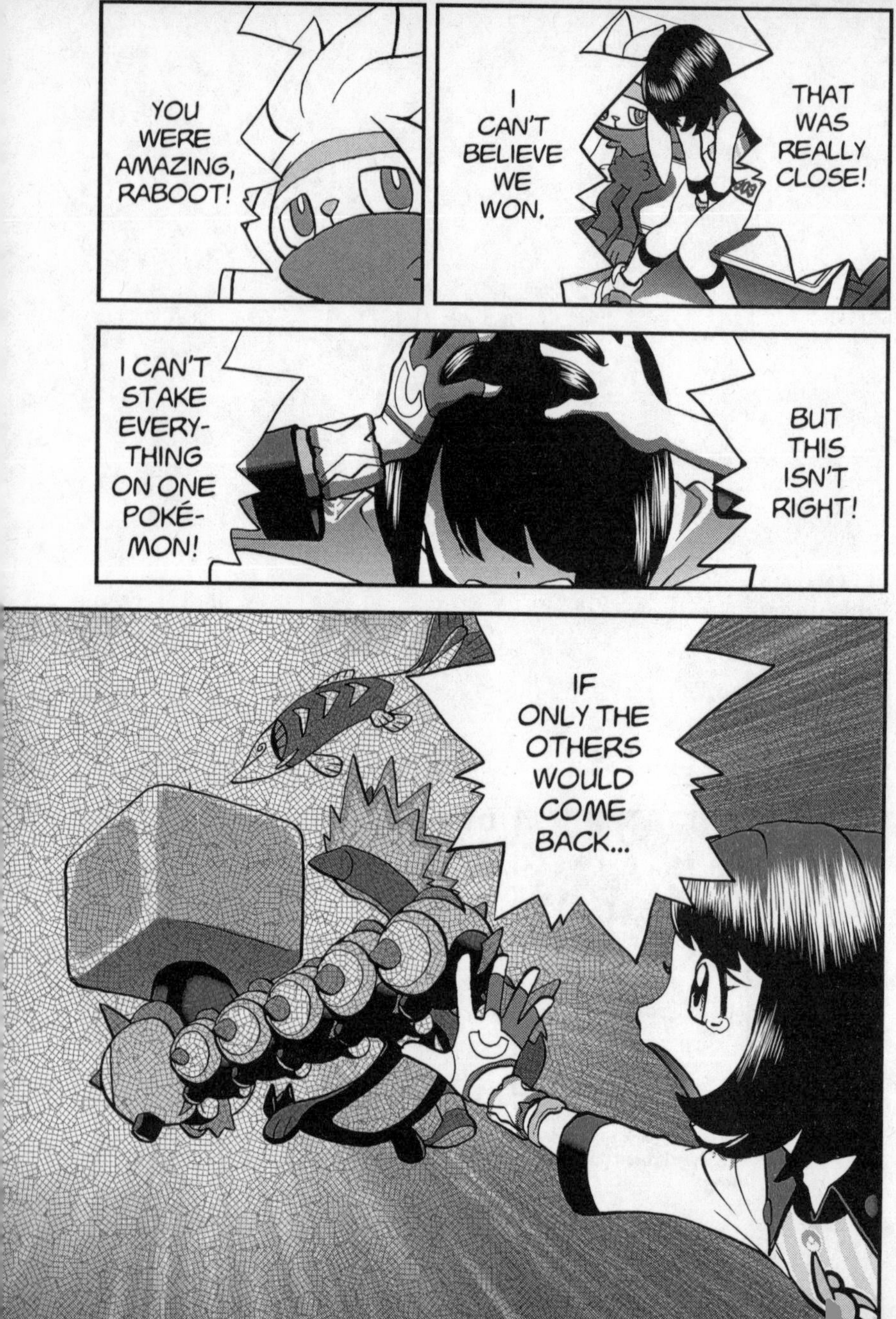
THAT WAS REALLY CLOSE!
I CAN'T BELIEVE WE WON.
YOU WERE AMAZING, RABOOT!
BUT THIS ISN'T RIGHT!
I CAN'T STAKE EVERYTHING ON ONE POKÉMON!
IF ONLY THE OTHERS WOULD COME BACK...

THE SECRETS OF DYNAMAX, PART 8

Dynamax Battle

There is an "only one Dynamaxing per battle" rule for official Gym battles, and there's a time limit too.

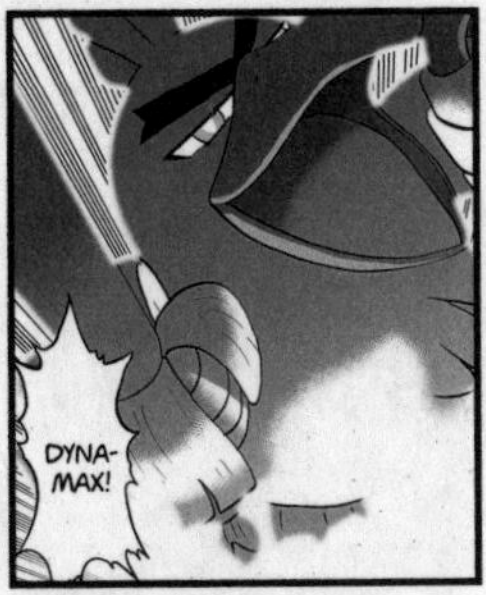
DYNA-
MAX!

▲ A Dynamaxed Pokémon will shrink back to ordinary size after it uses three moves.

Adventure 10 Blazing!! Bede's Feelings

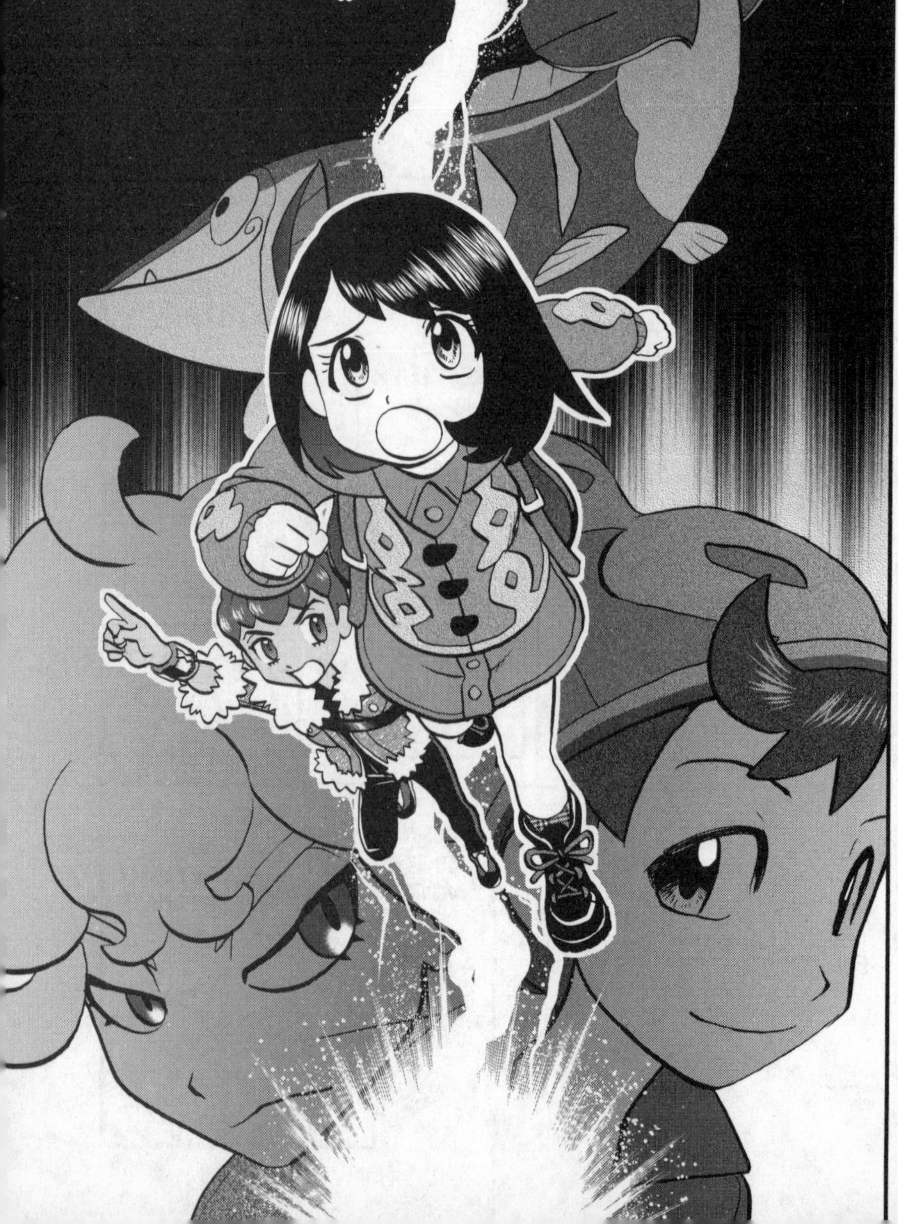

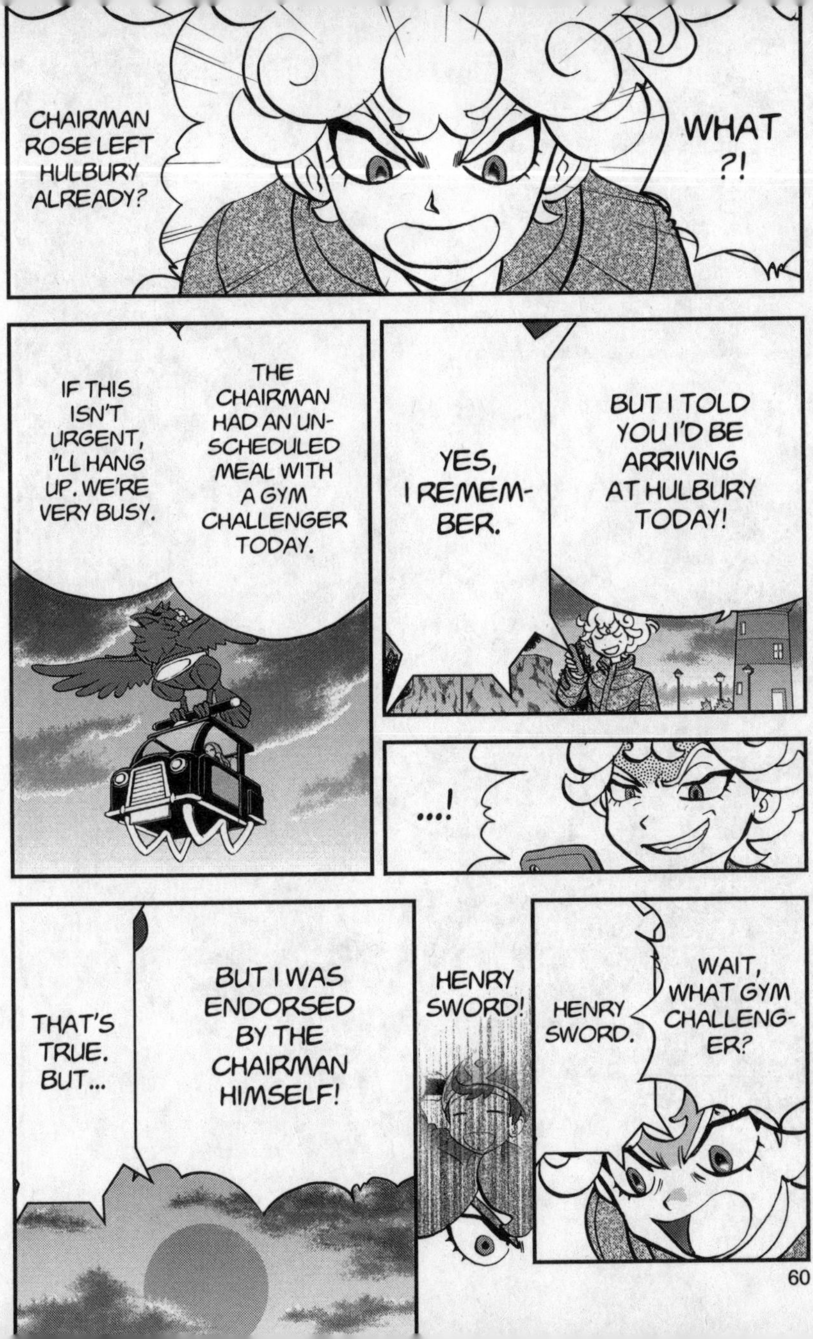
WHAT ?!
CHAIRMAN ROSE LEFT HULBURY ALREADY?
BUT I TOLD YOU I'D BE ARRIVING AT HULBURY TODAY!
YES, I REMEMBER.
...!
THE CHAIRMAN HAD AN UNSCHEDULED MEAL WITH A GYM CHALLENGER TODAY.
IF THIS ISN'T URGENT, I'LL HANG UP. WE'RE VERY BUSY.
WAIT, WHAT GYM CHALLENGER?
HENRY SWORD.
HENRY SWORD!
BUT I WAS ENDORSED BY THE CHAIRMAN HIMSELF!
THAT'S TRUE. BUT...

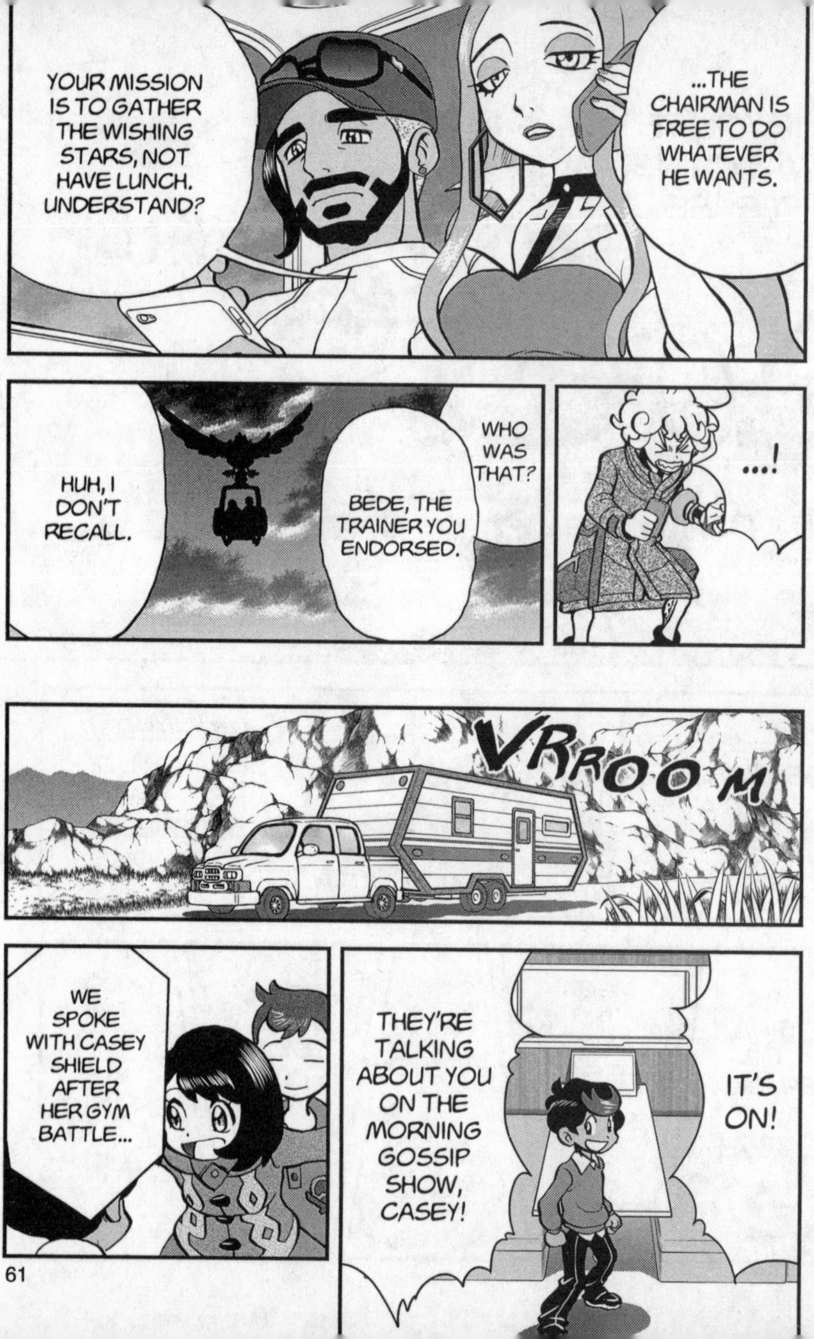
...THE CHAIRMAN IS FREE TO DO WHATEVER HE WANTS.
YOUR MISSION IS TO GATHER THE WISHING STARS, NOT HAVE LUNCH. UNDERSTAND?
...!
WHO WAS THAT?
BEDE, THE TRAINER YOU ENDORSED.
HUH, I DON'T RECALL.
VRROOM
IT'S ON!
THEY'RE TALKING ABOUT YOU ON THE MORNING GOSSIP SHOW, CASEY!
WE SPOKE WITH CASEY SHIELD AFTER HER GYM BATTLE...

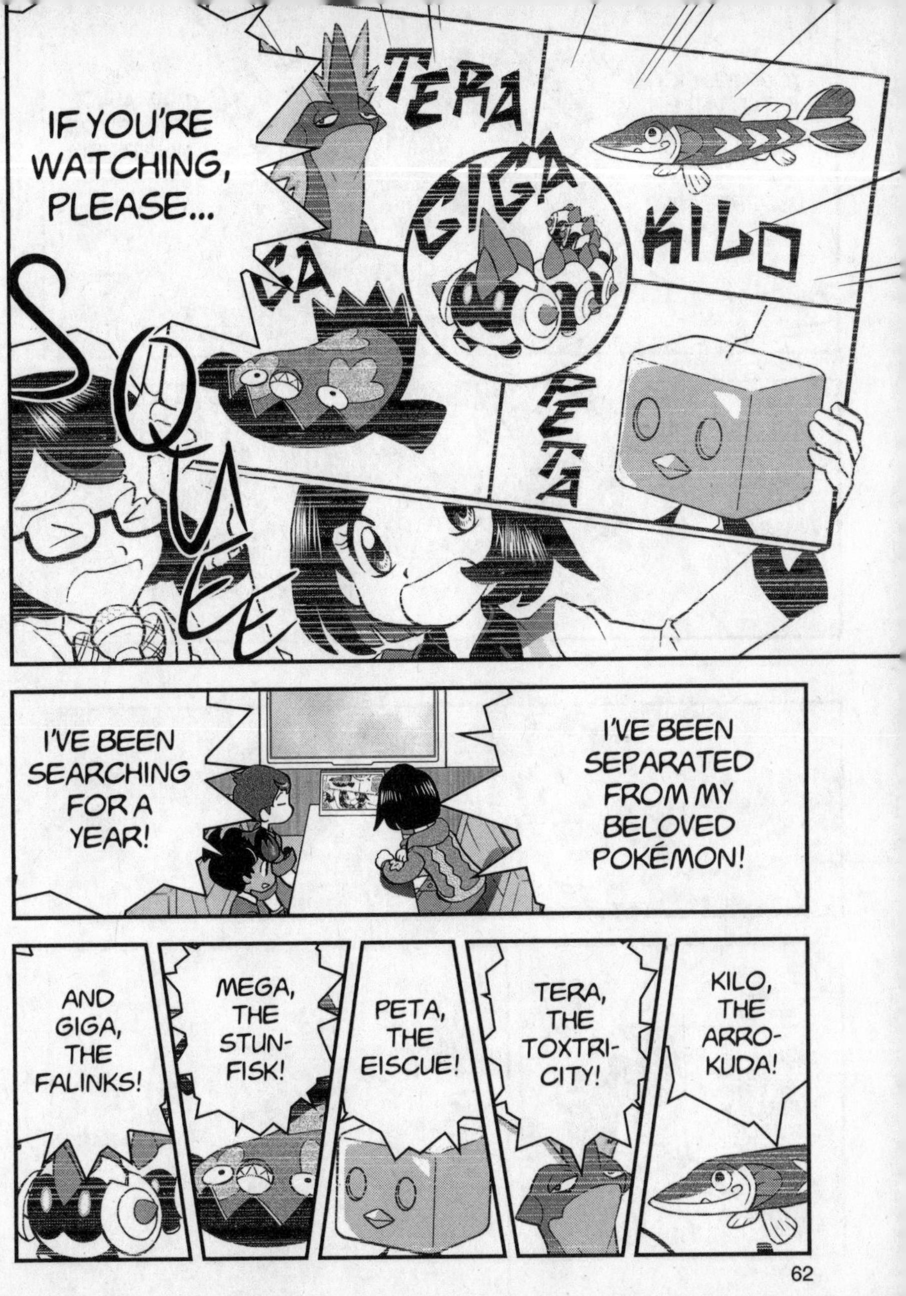
KILO
TERA
GIGA
PETA
GA
IF YOU'RE WATCHING, PLEASE...
SQUEE
I'VE BEEN SEPARATED FROM MY BELOVED POKÉMON!
I'VE BEEN SEARCHING FOR A YEAR!
KILO, THE ARRO-KUDA!
TERA, THE TOXTRI-CITY!
PETA, THE EISCUE!
MEGA, THE STUN-FISK!
AND GIGA, THE FALINKS!

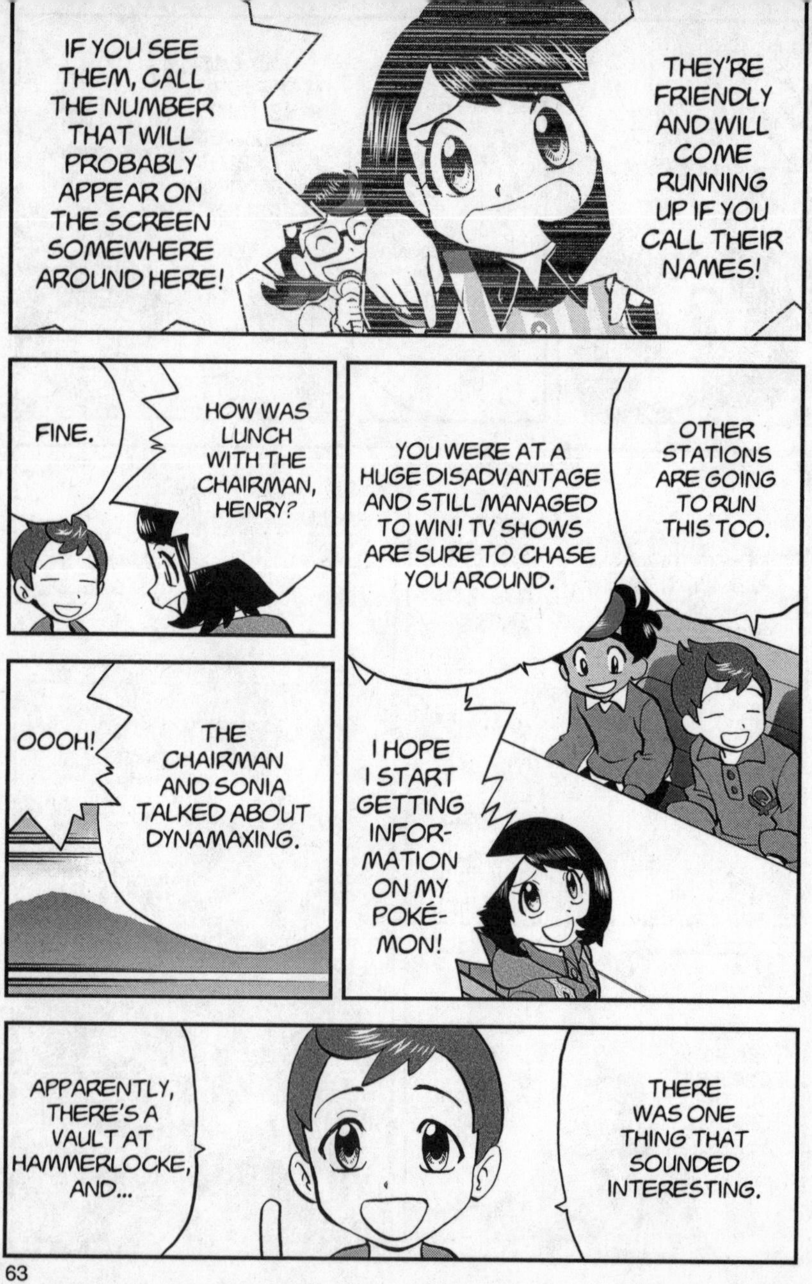
THEY'RE FRIENDLY AND WILL COME RUNNING UP IF YOU CALL THEIR NAMES!
IF YOU SEE THEM, CALL THE NUMBER THAT WILL PROBABLY APPEAR ON THE SCREEN SOMEWHERE AROUND HERE!
OTHER STATIONS ARE GOING TO RUN THIS TOO.
YOU WERE AT A HUGE DISADVANTAGE AND STILL MANAGED TO WIN! TV SHOWS ARE SURE TO CHASE YOU AROUND.
I HOPE I START GETTING INFOR-MATION ON MY POKÉ-MON!
HOW WAS LUNCH WITH THE CHAIRMAN, HENRY?
FINE.
THE CHAIRMAN AND SONIA TALKED ABOUT DYNAMAXING.
OOOH!
THERE WAS ONE THING THAT SOUNDED INTERESTING.
APPARENTLY, THERE'S A VAULT AT HAMMERLOCKE, AND...

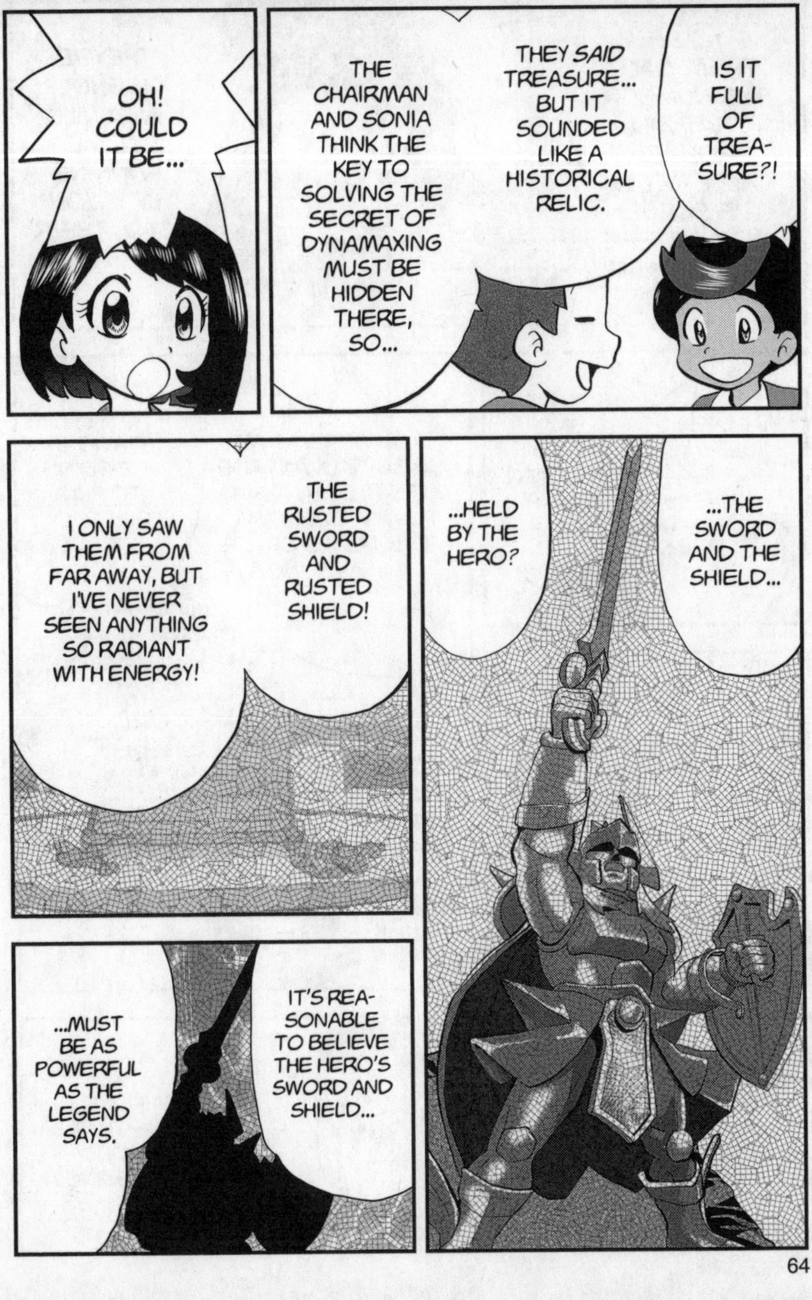
IS IT FULL OF TREASURE?!
THEY SAID TREASURE... BUT IT SOUNDED LIKE A HISTORICAL RELIC.
THE CHAIRMAN AND SONIA THINK THE KEY TO SOLVING THE SECRET OF DYNAMAXING MUST BE HIDDEN THERE, SO...
OH! COULD IT BE...
...THE SWORD AND THE SHIELD...
...HELD BY THE HERO?
THE RUSTED SWORD AND RUSTED SHIELD!
I ONLY SAW THEM FROM FAR AWAY, BUT I'VE NEVER SEEN ANYTHING SO RADIANT WITH ENERGY!
IT'S REASONABLE TO BELIEVE THE HERO'S SWORD AND SHIELD...
...MUST BE AS POWERFUL AS THE LEGEND SAYS.

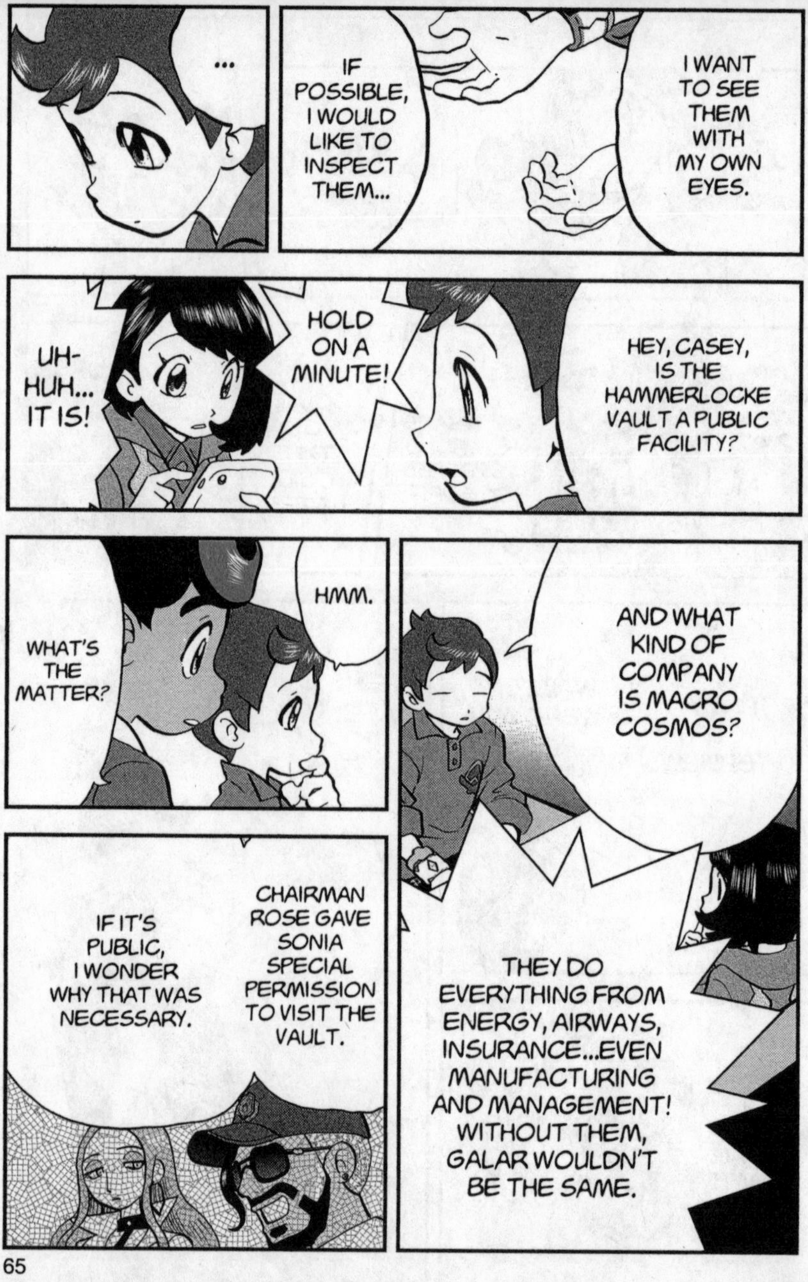
I WANT TO SEE THEM WITH MY OWN EYES.
IF POSSIBLE, I WOULD LIKE TO INSPECT THEM...
...
HEY, CASEY, IS THE HAMMERLOCKE VAULT A PUBLIC FACILITY?
HOLD ON A MINUTE!
UH-HUH... IT IS!
AND WHAT KIND OF COMPANY IS MACRO COSMOS?
THEY DO EVERYTHING FROM ENERGY, AIRWAYS, INSURANCE...EVEN MANUFACTURING AND MANAGEMENT! WITHOUT THEM, GALAR WOULDN'T BE THE SAME.
HMM.
WHAT'S THE MATTER?
CHAIRMAN ROSE GAVE SONIA SPECIAL PERMISSION TO VISIT THE VAULT.
IF IT'S PUBLIC, I WONDER WHY THAT WAS NECESSARY.

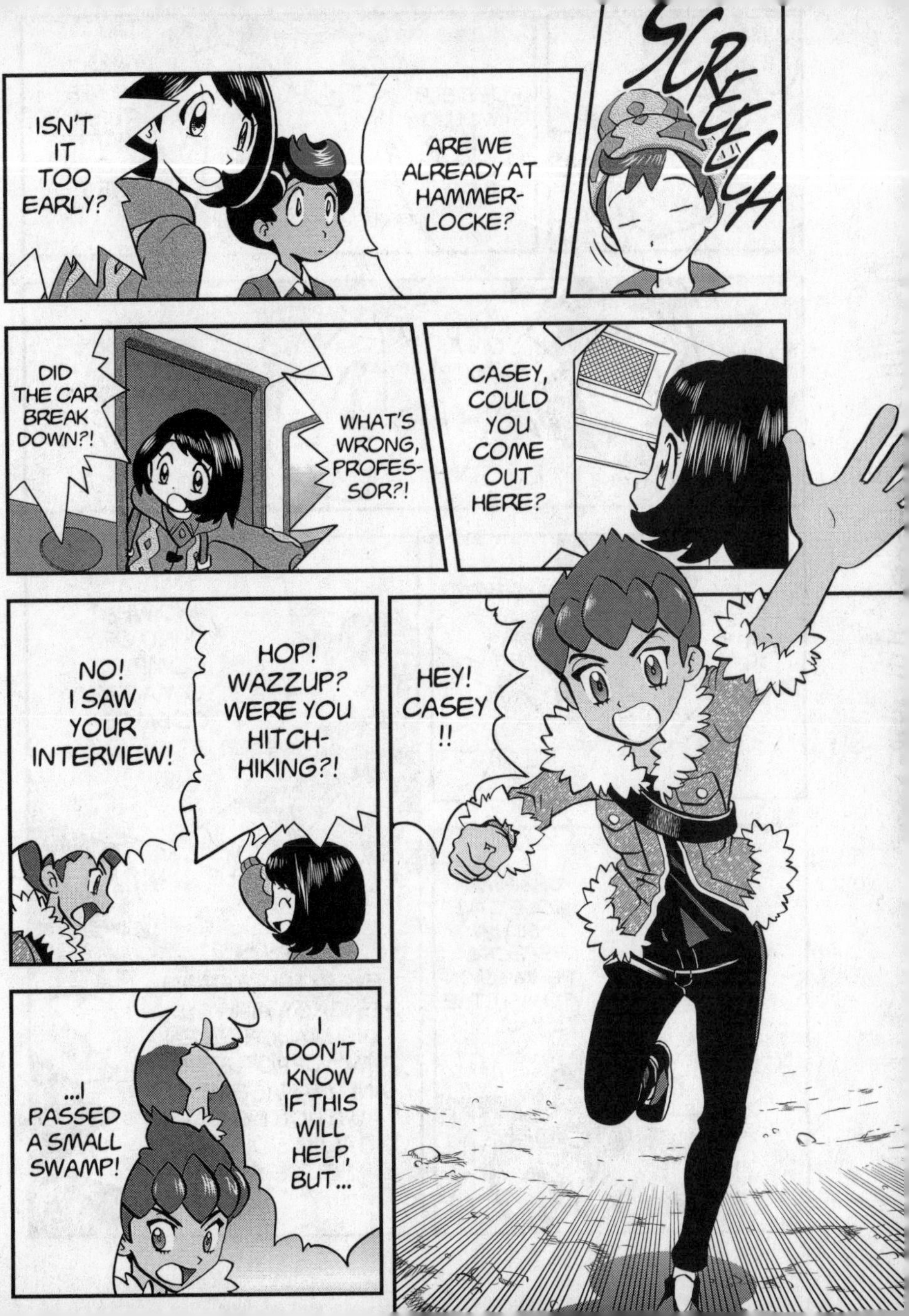
SCREECH
ARE WE ALREADY AT HAMMER-LOCKE?
ISN'T IT TOO EARLY?
CASEY, COULD YOU COME OUT HERE?
WHAT'S WRONG, PROFES-SOR?!
DID THE CAR BREAK DOWN?!
HEY! CASEY!!
HOP! WAZZUP? WERE YOU HITCH-HIKING?!
NO! I SAW YOUR INTERVIEW!
I DON'T KNOW IF THIS WILL HELP, BUT...
...I PASSED A SMALL SWAMP!

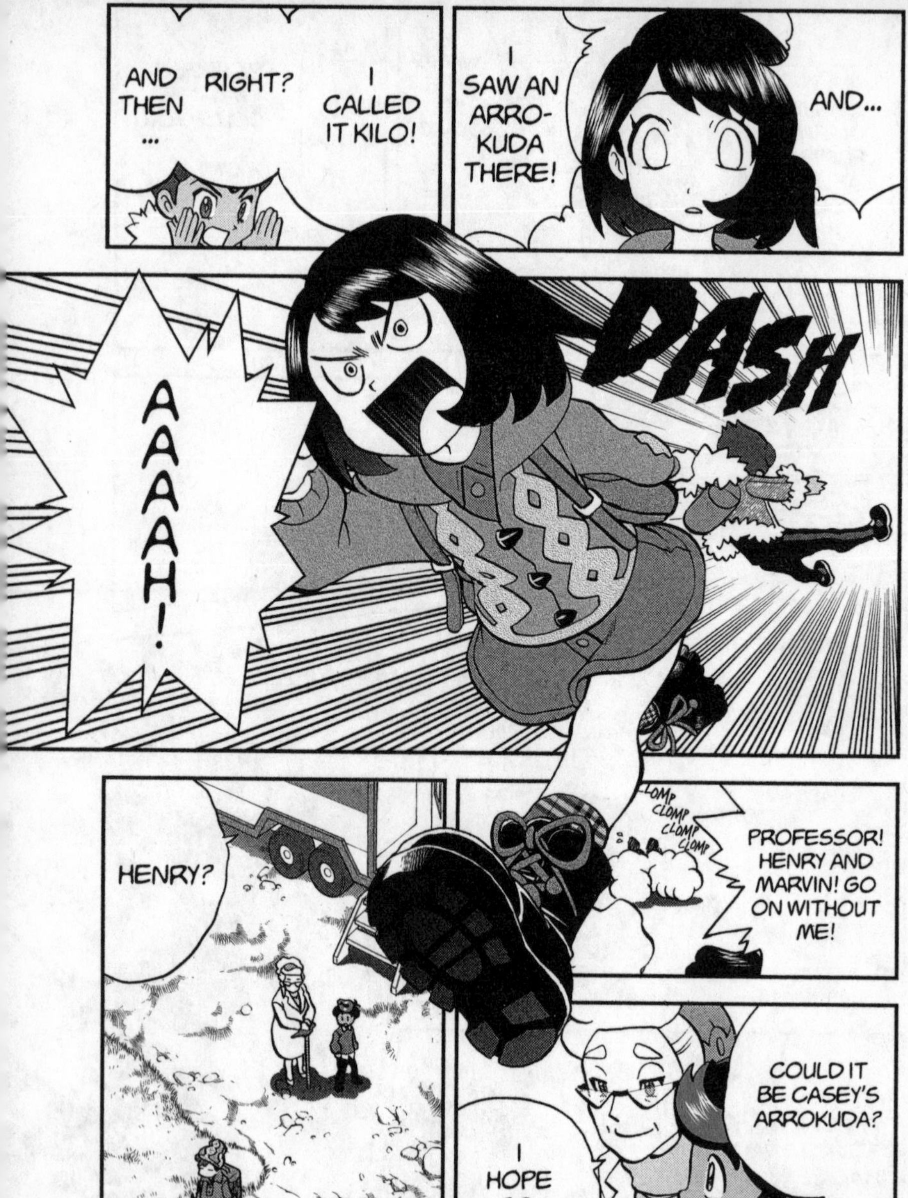
AND...
I SAW AN ARRO-KUDA THERE!
I CALLED IT KILO!
RIGHT?
AND THEN ...
DASH
AAAAAH!
CLOMP CLOMP CLOMP CLOMP
PROFESSOR! HENRY AND MARVIN! GO ON WITHOUT ME!
COULD IT BE CASEY'S ARROKUDA?
I HOPE SO.
HENRY?

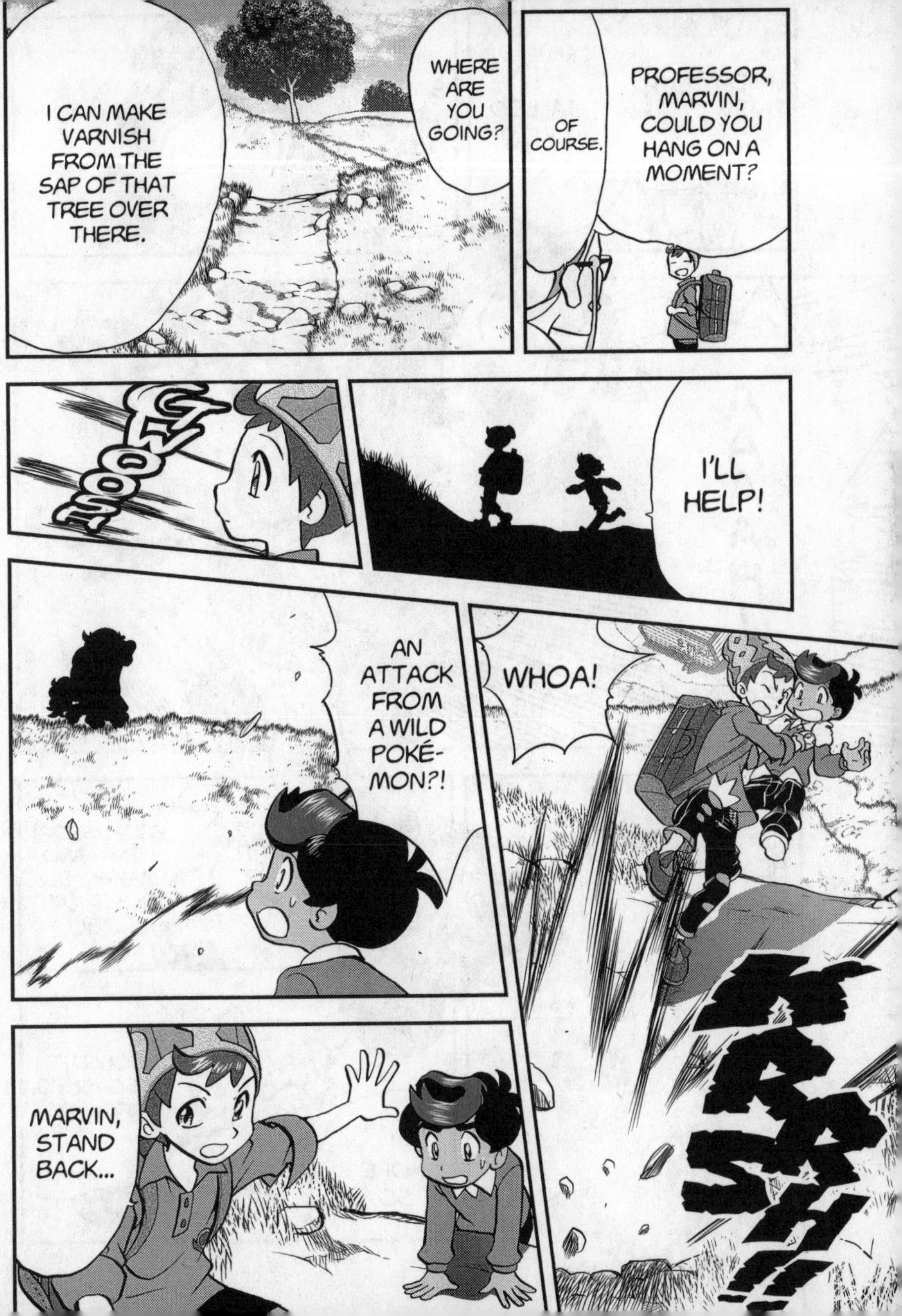
PROFESSOR, MARVIN, COULD YOU HANG ON A MOMENT?
OF COURSE.
WHERE ARE YOU GOING?
I CAN MAKE VARNISH FROM THE SAP OF THAT TREE OVER THERE.
I'LL HELP!
WHOA!
AN ATTACK FROM A WILD POKÉMON?!
MARVIN, STAND BACK...

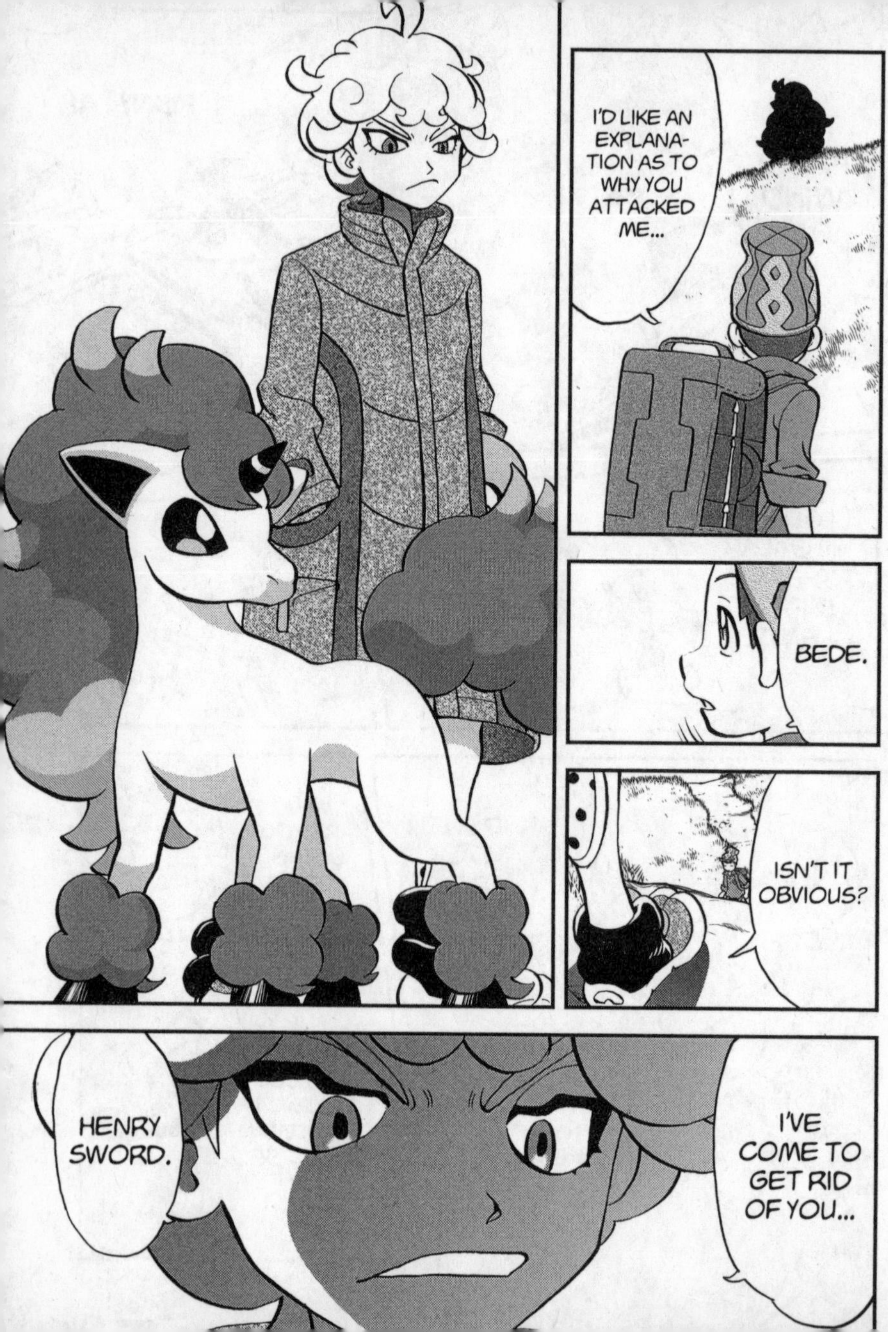
I'D LIKE AN EXPLANATION AS TO WHY YOU ATTACKED ME...
BEDE.
ISN'T IT OBVIOUS?
I'VE COME TO GET RID OF YOU...
HENRY SWORD.

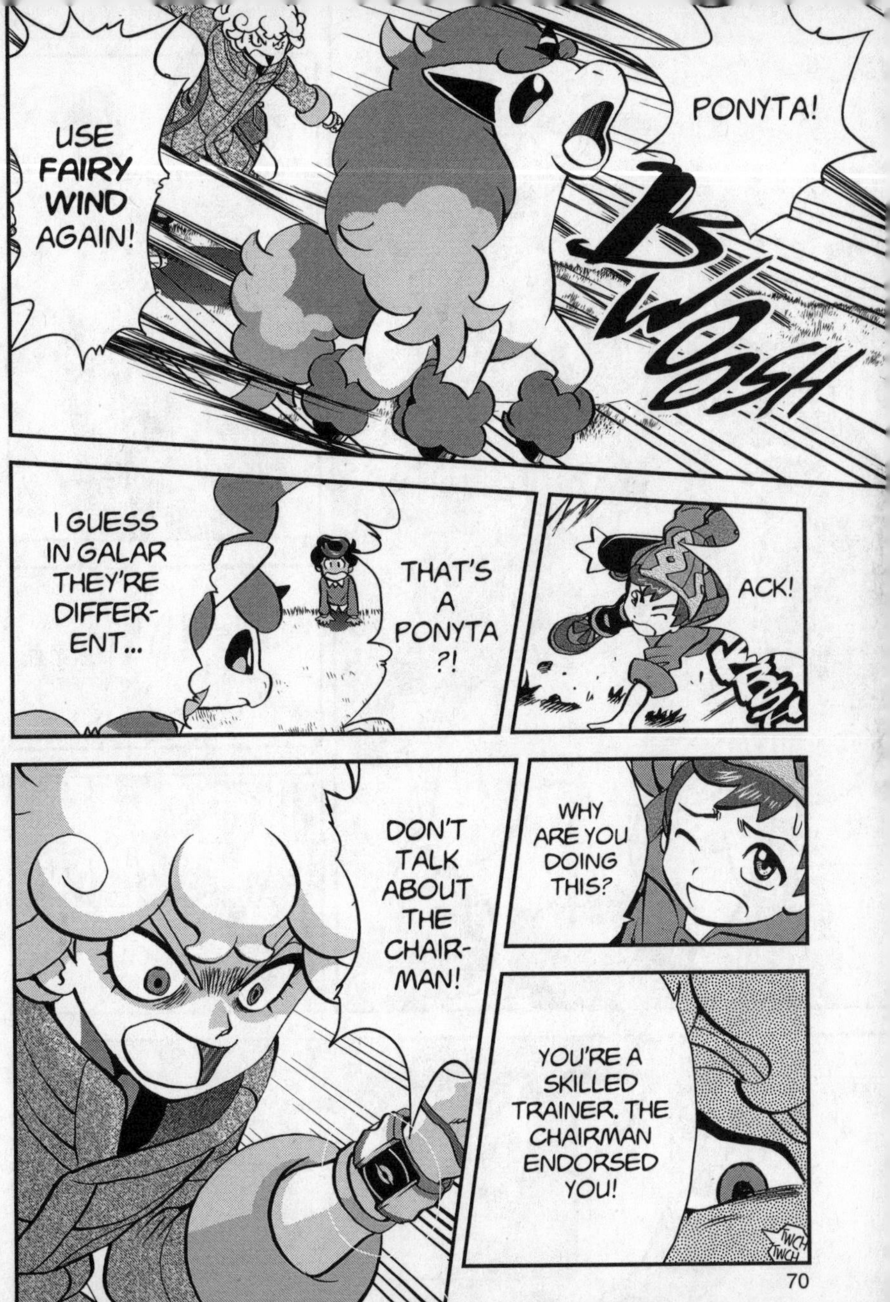
PONYTA!
BWOOSH
USE FAIRY WIND AGAIN!
ACK!
THAT'S A PONYTA?!
I GUESS IN GALAR THEY'RE DIFFER-ENT...
WHY ARE YOU DOING THIS?
YOU'RE A SKILLED TRAINER. THE CHAIRMAN ENDORSED YOU!
TWCH TWCH
DON'T TALK ABOUT THE CHAIR-MAN!

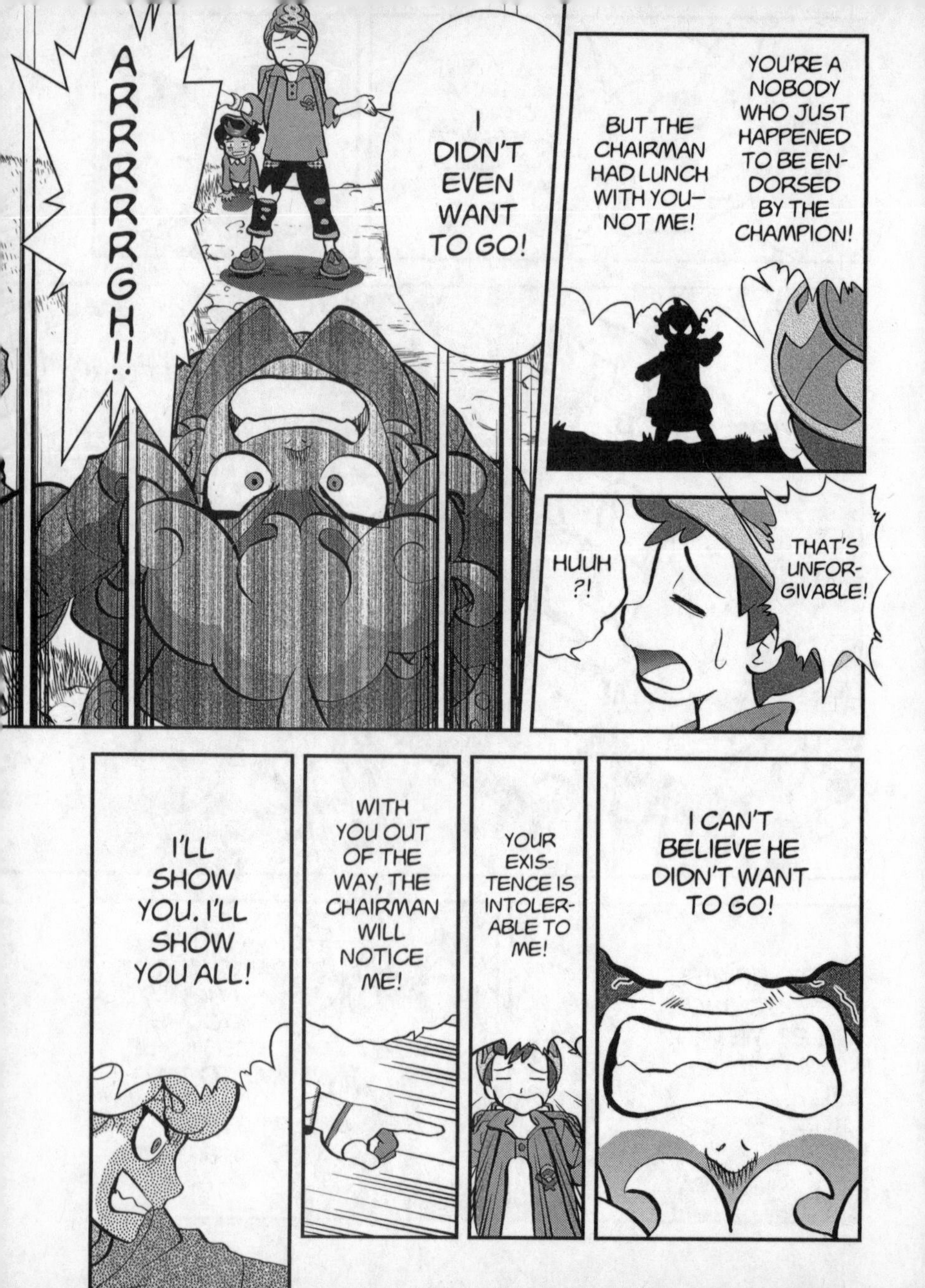
YOU'RE A NOBODY WHO JUST HAPPENED TO BE EN-DORSED BY THE CHAMPION!
BUT THE CHAIRMAN HAD LUNCH WITH YOU—NOT ME!
THAT'S UNFOR-GIVABLE!
HUUH ?!
I DIDN'T EVEN WANT TO GO!
ARRRRRGH!!
I CAN'T BELIEVE HE DIDN'T WANT TO GO!
YOUR EXIS-TENCE IS INTOLER-ABLE TO ME!
WITH YOU OUT OF THE WAY, THE CHAIRMAN WILL NOTICE ME!
I'LL SHOW YOU. I'LL SHOW YOU ALL!

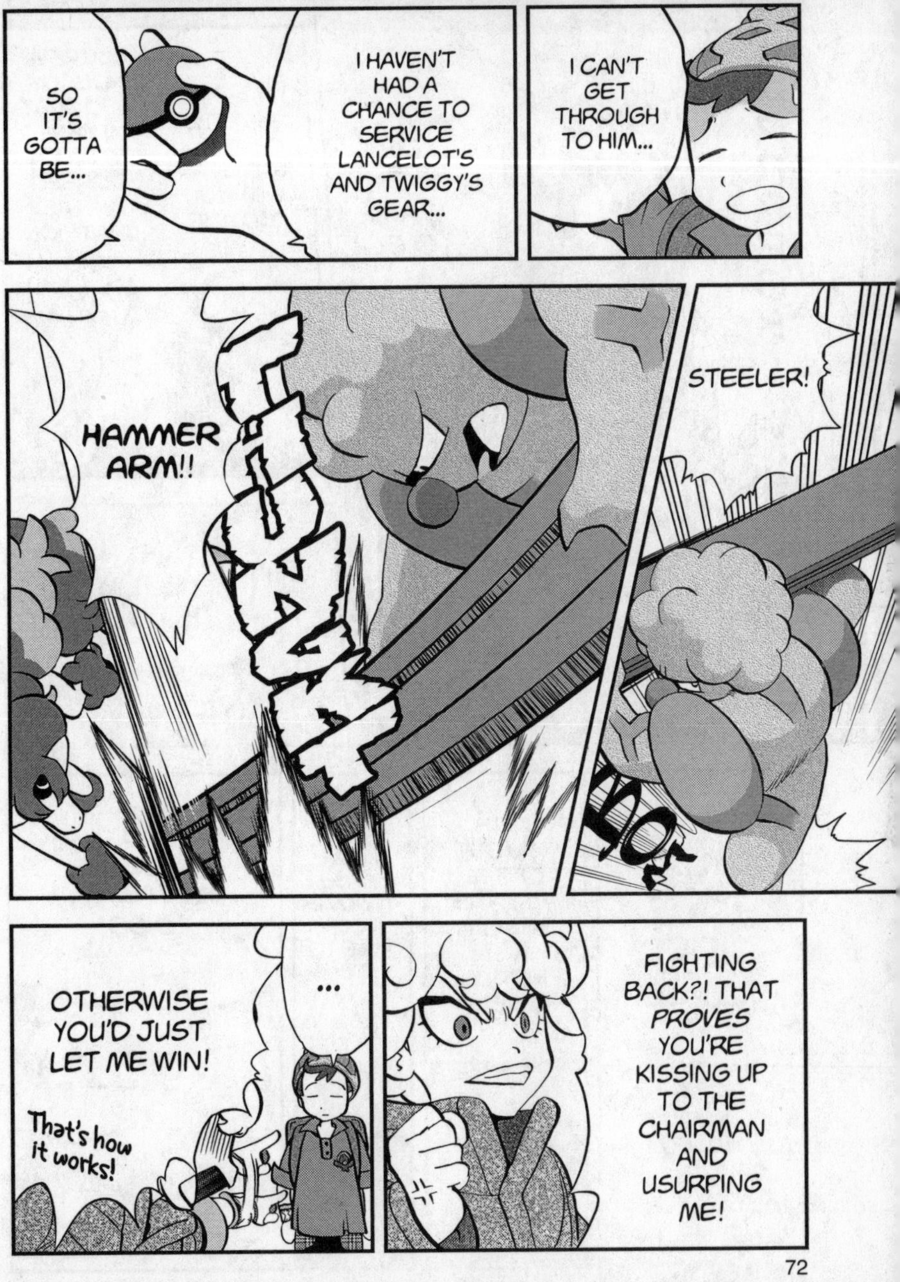
I CAN'T GET THROUGH TO HIM...
I HAVEN'T HAD A CHANCE TO SERVICE LANCELOT'S AND TWIGGY'S GEAR...
SO IT'S GOTTA BE...
STEELER!
HAMMER ARM!!
FIGHTING BACK?! THAT *PROVES* YOU'RE KISSING UP TO THE CHAIRMAN AND USURPING ME!
...
OTHERWISE YOU'D JUST LET ME WIN!
That's how it works!

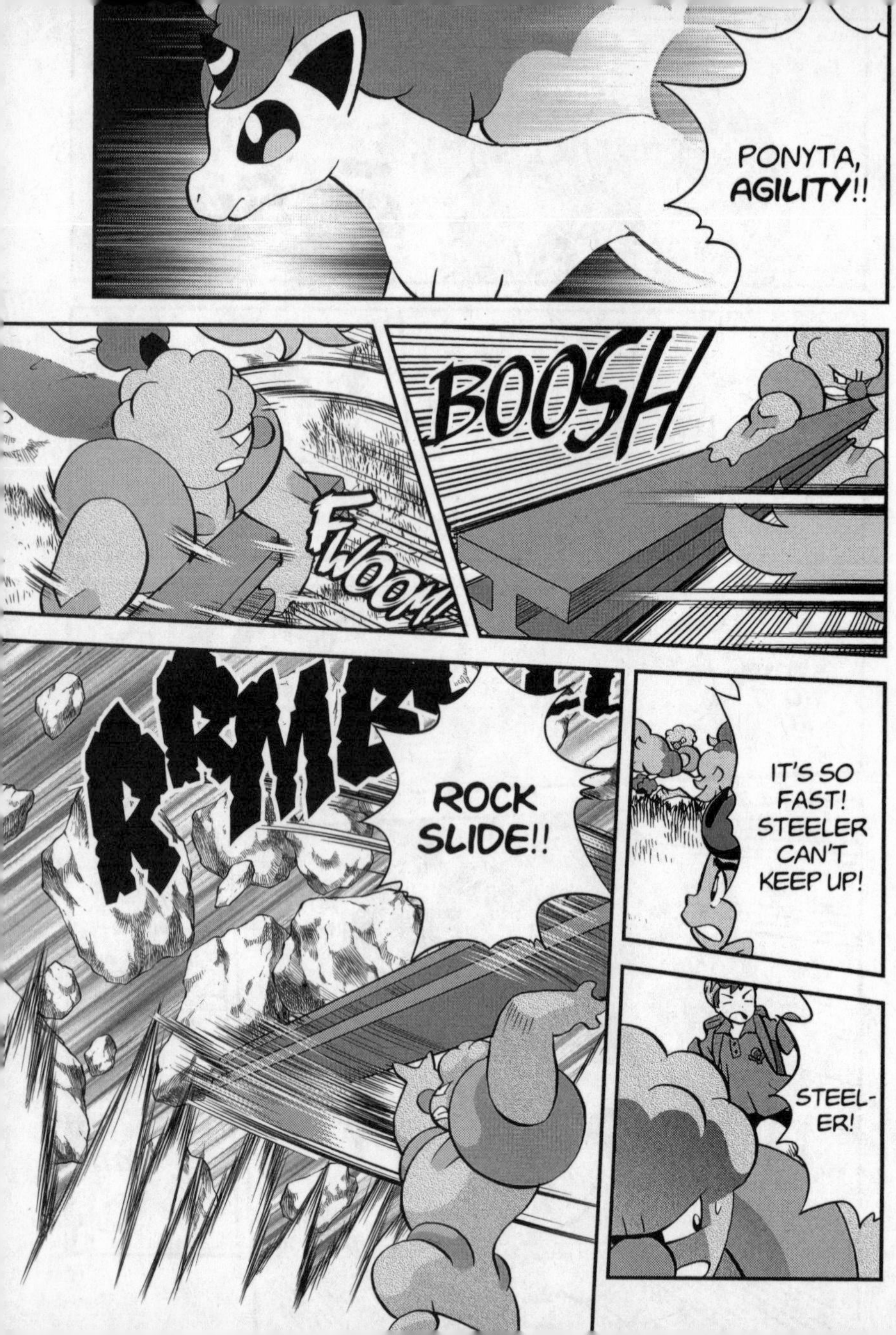
PONYTA, AGILITY!!
BOOSH
FWOOM!
IT'S SO FAST! STEELER CAN'T KEEP UP!
STEEL-ER!
ROCK SLIDE!!

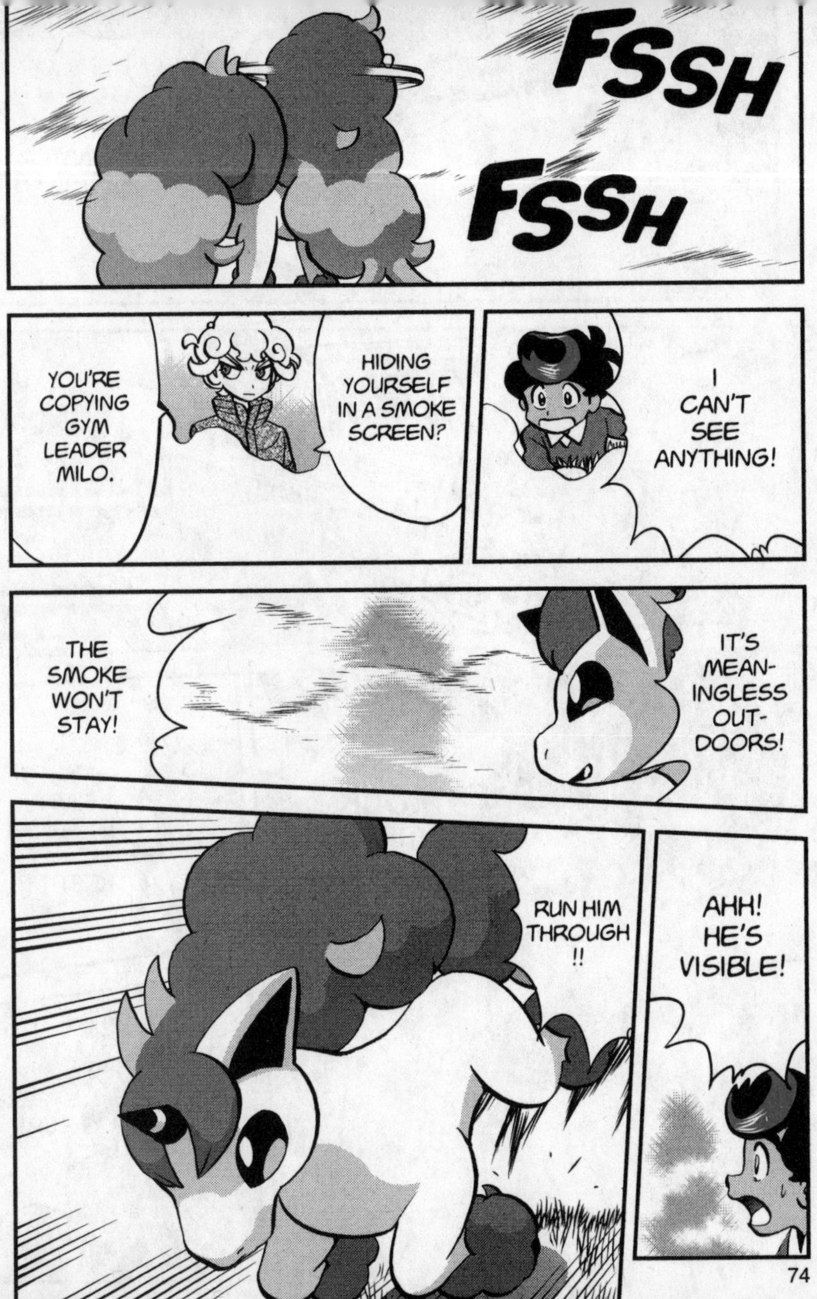
FSSH
FSSH
I CAN'T SEE ANYTHING!
HIDING YOURSELF IN A SMOKE SCREEN?
YOU'RE COPYING GYM LEADER MILO.
IT'S MEAN-INGLESS OUT-DOORS!
THE SMOKE WON'T STAY!
AHH! HE'S VISIBLE!
RUN HIM THROUGH!!

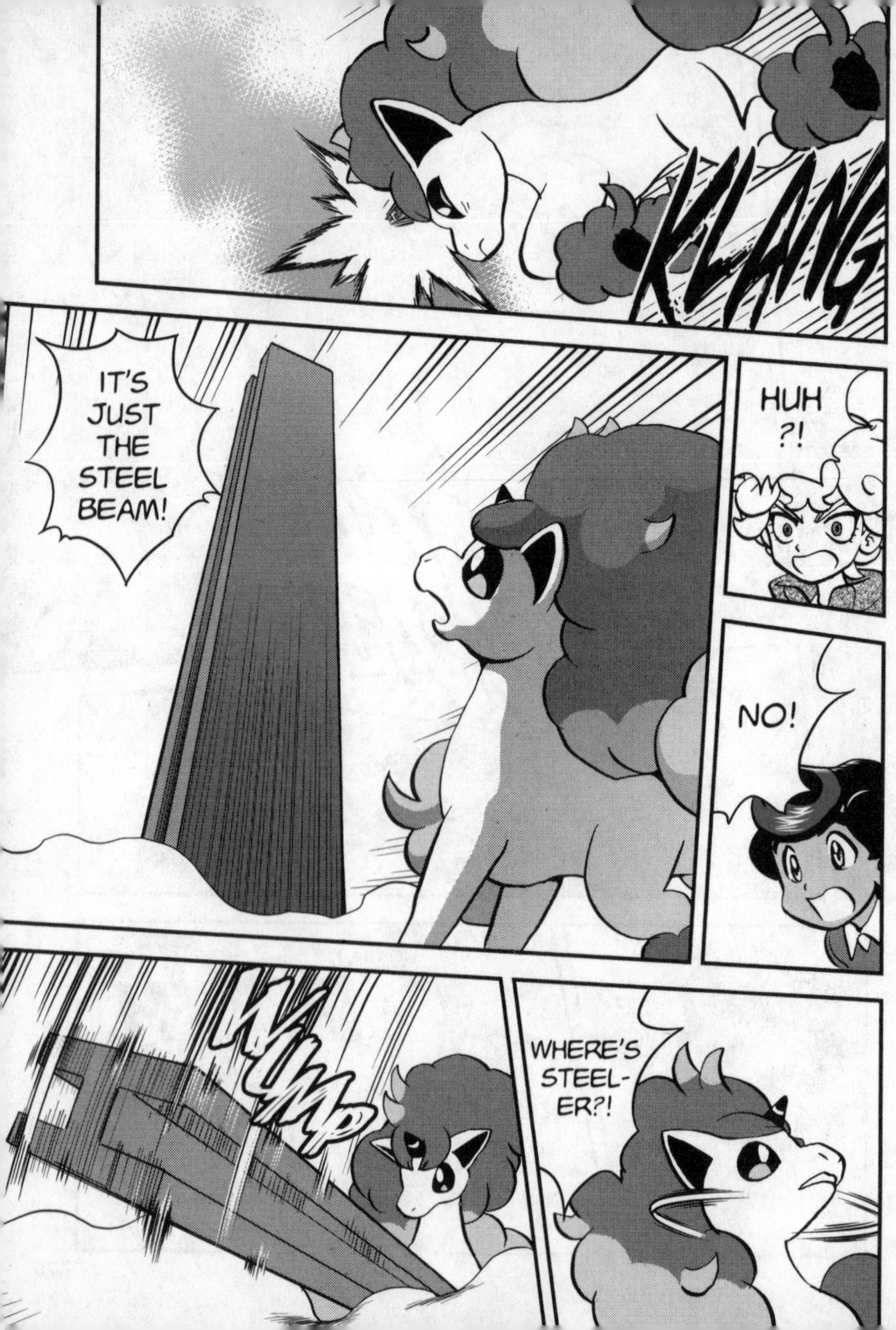
KLANG
HUH ?!
NO!
IT'S JUST THE STEEL BEAM!
WHERE'S STEELER?!
WUMP

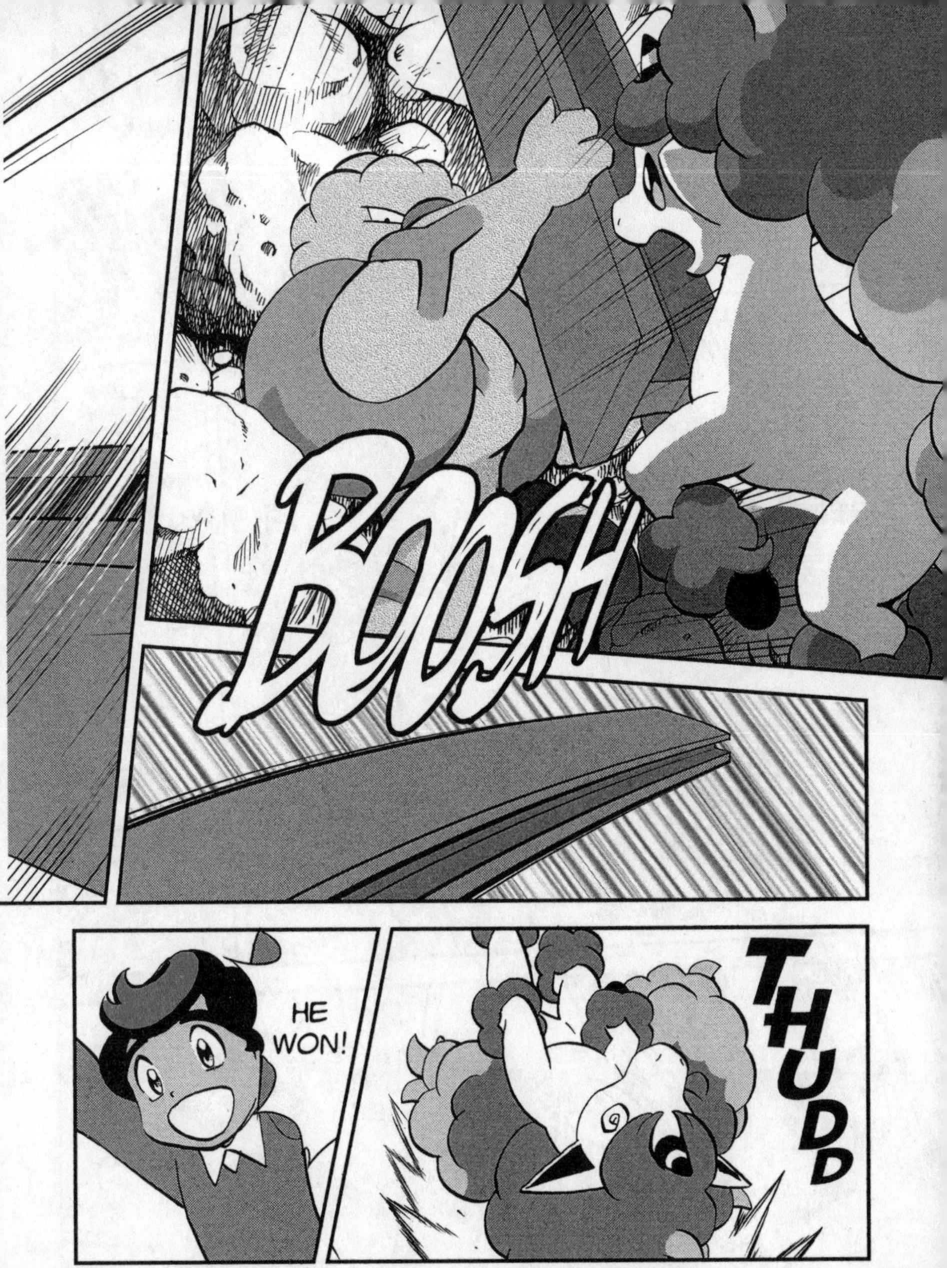
BOOSH
THUDD
HE WON!

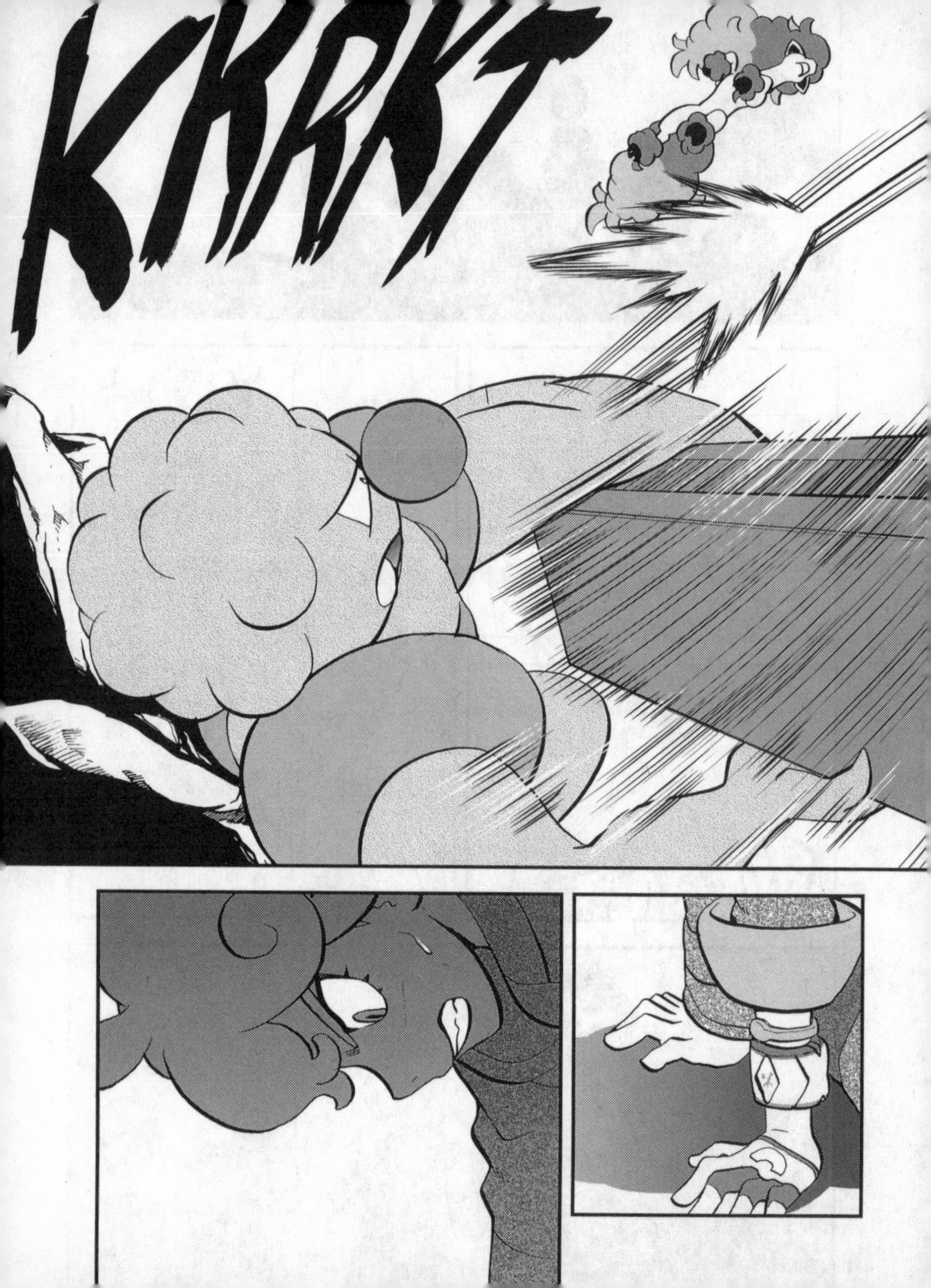
KKRKT

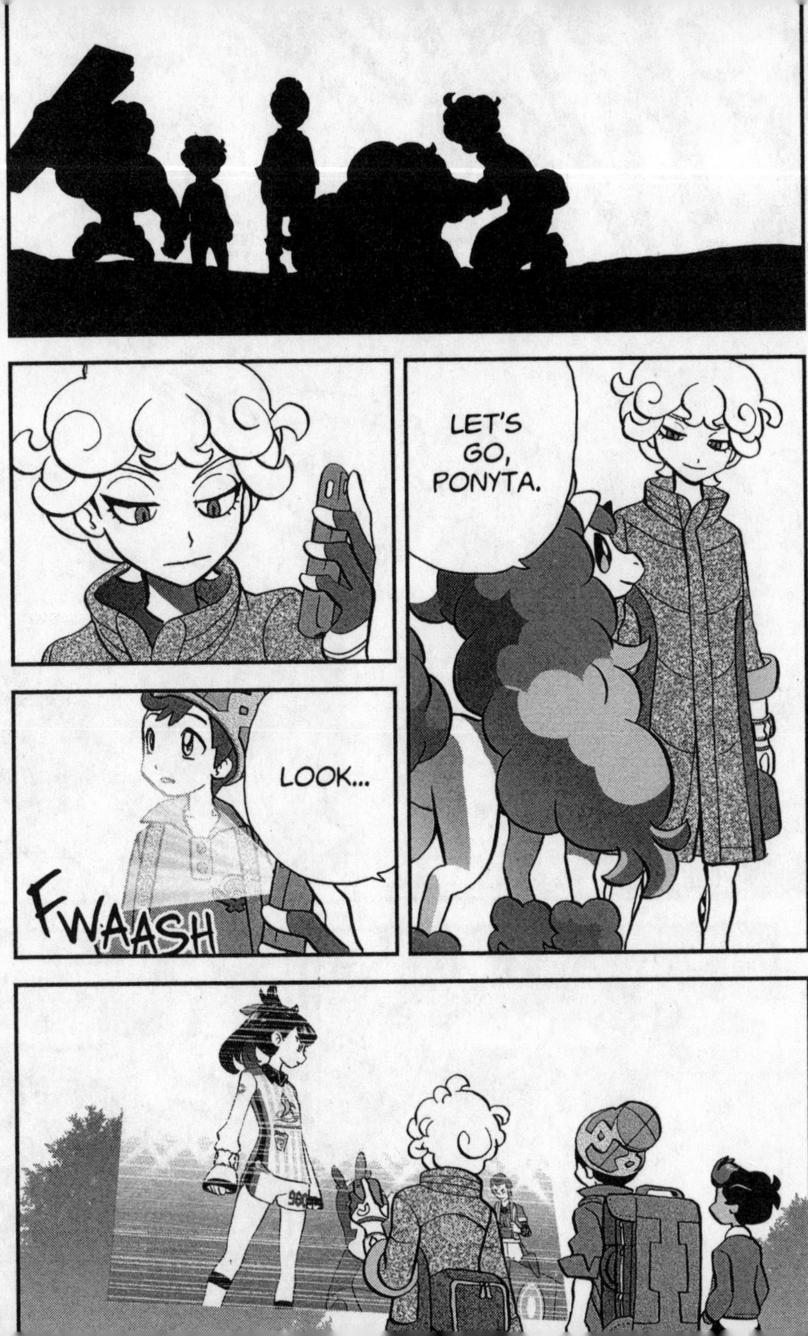
LET'S GO, PONYTA.
LOOK...
FWAASH

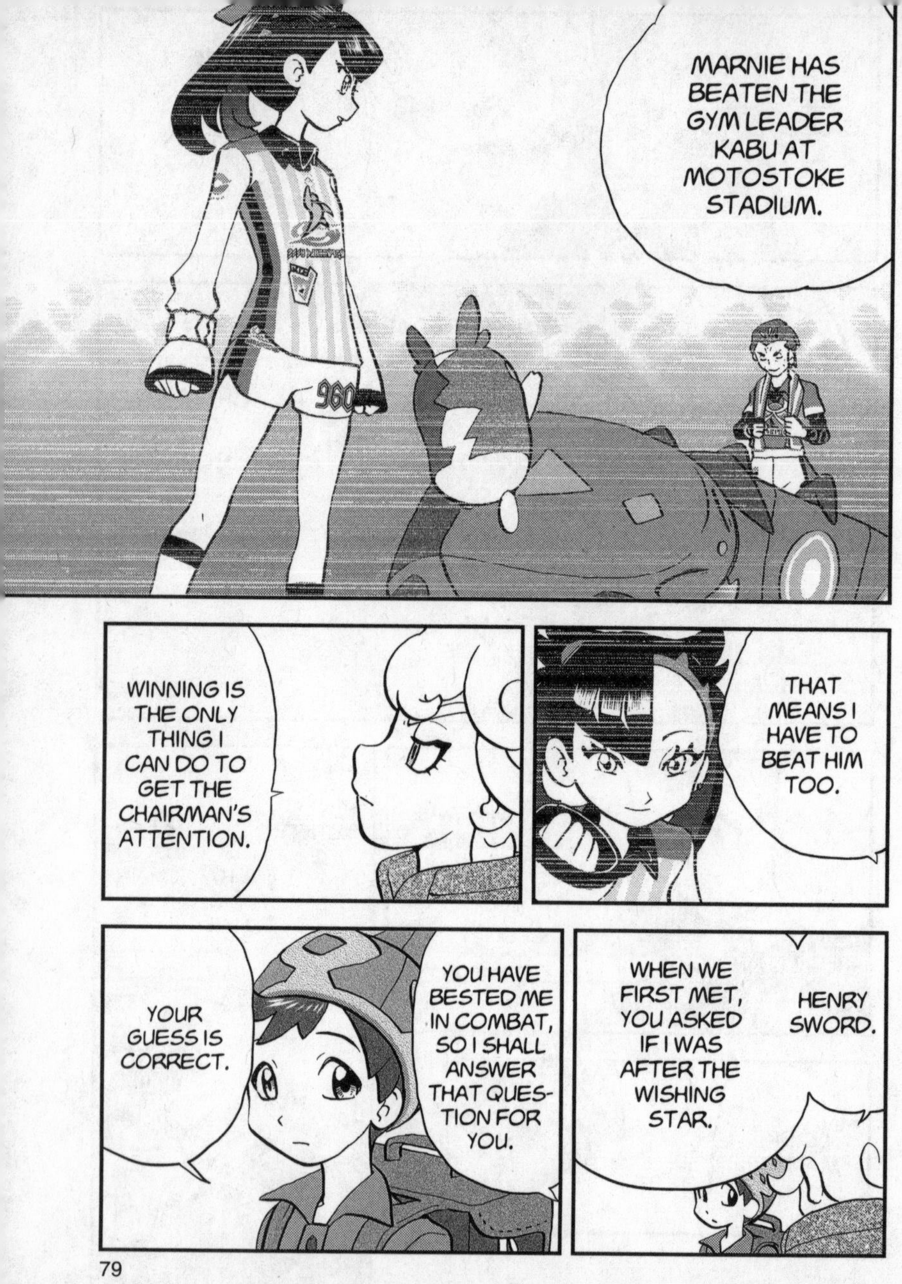
MARNIE HAS BEATEN THE GYM LEADER KABU AT MOTOSTOKE STADIUM.
THAT MEANS I HAVE TO BEAT HIM TOO.
WINNING IS THE ONLY THING I CAN DO TO GET THE CHAIRMAN'S ATTENTION.
HENRY SWORD.
WHEN WE FIRST MET, YOU ASKED IF I WAS AFTER THE WISHING STAR.
YOU HAVE BESTED ME IN COMBAT, SO I SHALL ANSWER THAT QUES-TION FOR YOU.
YOUR GUESS IS CORRECT.

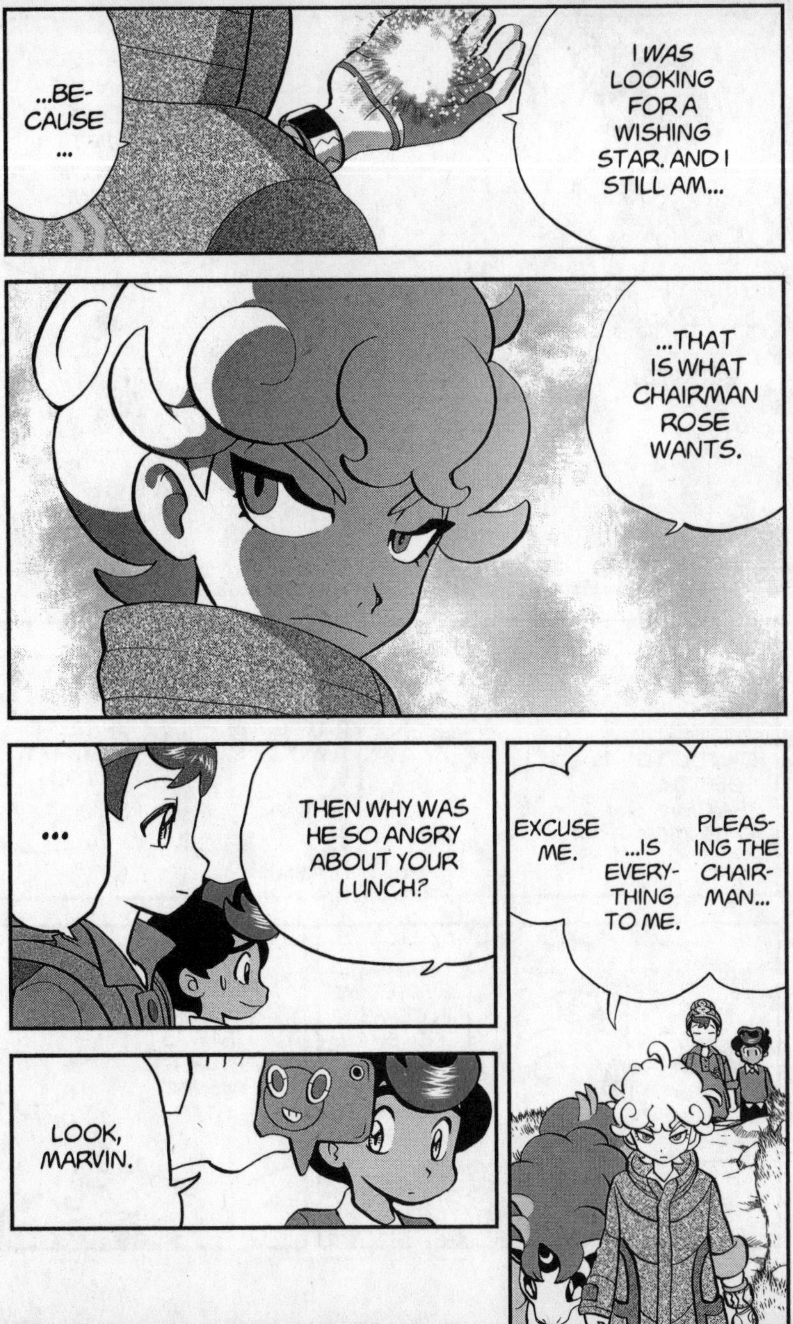
I WAS LOOKING FOR A WISHING STAR. AND I STILL AM...
...BE-CAUSE ...
...THAT IS WHAT CHAIRMAN ROSE WANTS.
PLEAS-ING THE CHAIR-MAN...
...IS EVERY-THING TO ME.
EXCUSE ME.
THEN WHY WAS HE SO ANGRY ABOUT YOUR LUNCH?
...
LOOK, MARVIN.

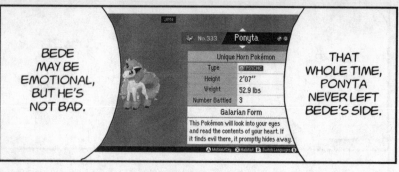

BEDE MAY BE EMOTIONAL, BUT HE'S NOT BAD.

No.333 Ponyta

Unique Horn Pokémon

Type	PSYCHIC
Height	2'07"
Weight	52.9 lbs
Number Battled	3

Galarian Form

This Pokémon will look into your eyes and read the contents of your heart. If it finds evil there, it promptly hides away.

THAT WHOLE TIME, PONYTA NEVER LEFT BEDE'S SIDE.

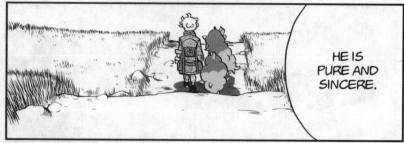

HE IS PURE AND SINCERE.

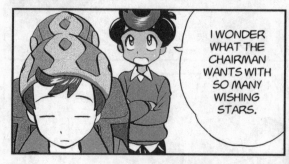

I WONDER WHAT THE CHAIRMAN WANTS WITH SO MANY WISHING STARS.

PROFESSOR MAGNOLIA WILL GET WORRIED.

SO LET'S GATHER THE TREE SAP AND GO BACK.

BUT IN THAT CASE, ONE GYM CHALLENGER WOULDN'T BE ENOUGH...

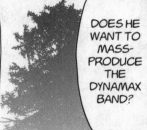

DOES HE WANT TO MASS-PRODUCE THE DYNAMAX BAND?

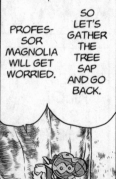

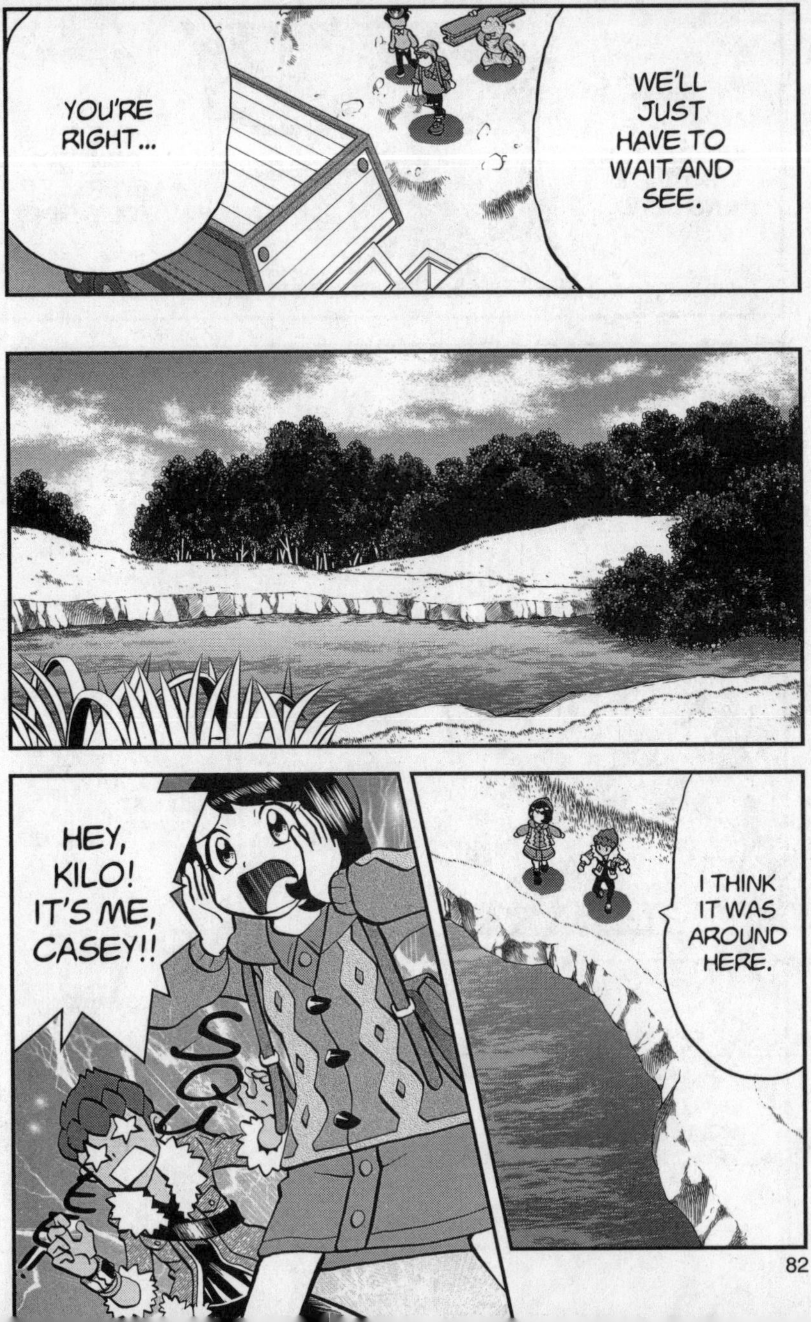
WE'LL JUST HAVE TO WAIT AND SEE.
YOU'RE RIGHT...
I THINK IT WAS AROUND HERE.
HEY, KILO! IT'S ME, CASEY!!
SQUE

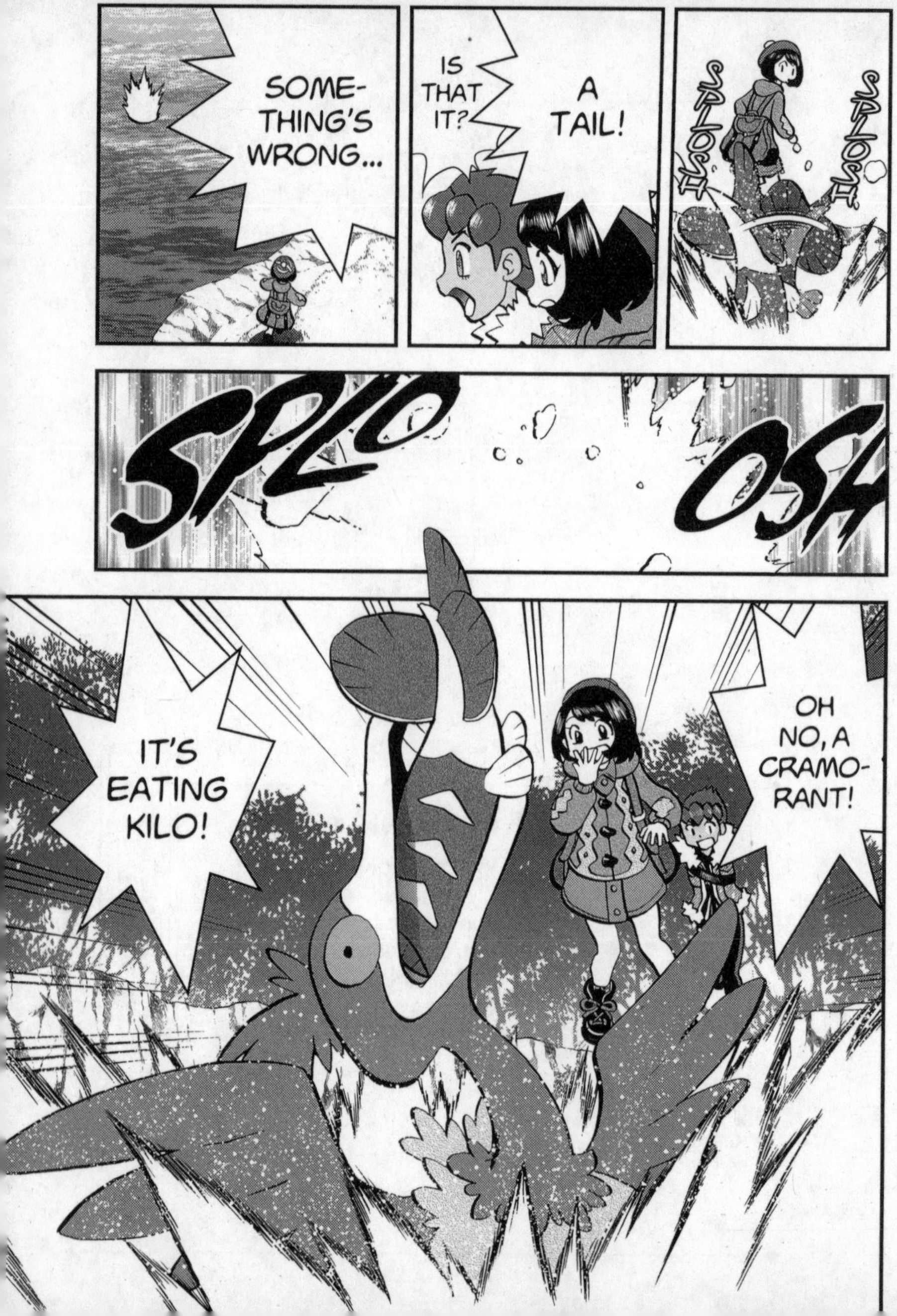
SPLOSH
SPLOSH
A TAIL!
IS THAT IT?
SOME-THING'S WRONG...
SPLOOSH
OH NO, A CRAMO-RANT!
IT'S EATING KILO!

THE SECRETS OF DYNAMAX, PART 9

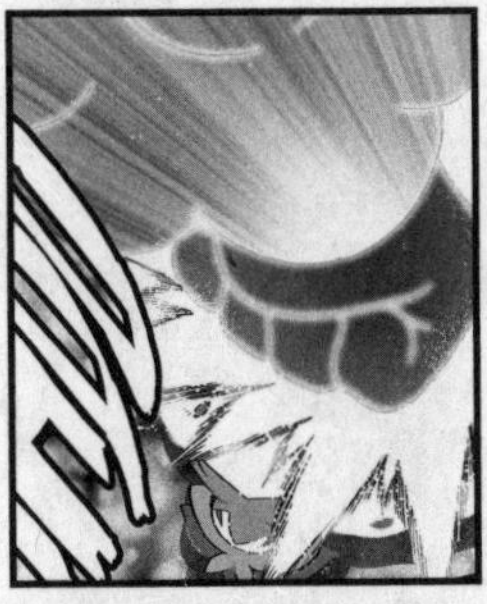

▲ Brick Break becomes Max Knuckle.

Max Move

When a Pokémon is Dynamaxed, moves become Max Moves, which are far more powerful. There are 19 Max Moves for Trainers to discover!

Hidenori Kusaka is the writer for *Pokémon Adventures*. Running continuously for over 20 years, *Pokémon Adventures* is the only manga series to completely cover all the *Pokémon* games and has become one of the most popular series of all time. In addition to writing manga, he also edits children's books and plans mixed-media projects for Shogakukan's children's magazines. He uses the Pokémon Electrode as his author portrait.

Satoshi Yamamoto is the artist for *Pokémon Adventures*, which he began working on in 2001, starting with volume 10. Yamamoto launched his manga career in 1993 with the horror-action title *Kimen Senshi*, which ran in Shogakukan's *Weekly Shonen Sunday* magazine, followed by the series *Kaze no Denshosha*. Yamamoto's favorite manga creators/artists include FUJIKO F FUJIO (*Doraemon*), Yukinobu Hoshino (*2001 Nights*) and Katsuhiro Otomo (*Akira*). He loves films, monsters, detective novels and punk rock music. He uses the Pokémon Swalot as his artist portrait.

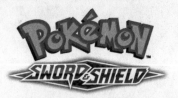

**Pokémon: Sword & Shield
Volume 3
VIZ Media Edition**

Story by HIDENORI KUSAKA
Art by SATOSHI YAMAMOTO

©2022 Pokémon.
©1995–2020 Nintendo / Creatures Inc. / GAME FREAK inc.
TM, ®, and character names are trademarks of Nintendo.
POCKET MONSTERS SPECIAL SWORD SHIELD Vol. 2
by Hidenori KUSAKA, Satoshi YAMAMOTO
© 2020 Hidenori KUSAKA, Satoshi YAMAMOTO
All rights reserved.
Original Japanese edition published by SHOGAKUKAN.
English translation rights in the United States of America, Canada, the United Kingdom,
Ireland, Australia and New Zealand arranged with SHOGAKUKAN.

Original Cover Design—Hiroyuki KAWASOME (grafio)

Translation—Tetsuichiro Miyaki
English Adaptation—Molly Tanzer
Touch-Up & Lettering—Annaliese "Ace" Christman
Design—Alice Lewis
Editor—Joel Enos

The stories, characters and incidents mentioned
in this publication are entirely fictional.

Printed in the U.S.A.

Published by VIZ Media, LLC
P.O. Box 77010
San Francisco, CA 94107

10 9 8 7 6 5 4 3 2 1
First printing, April 2022

W9-CEI-820

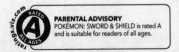

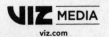
viz.com